The Last Stand

MARYANN BOUCO

WESTBOW
PRESS
A DIVISION OF THOMAS NELSON
& ZONDERVAN

Copyright © 2015 Maryann Bouco.

All rights reserved. No part of this book may be used or reproduced by any means, graphic, electronic, or mechanical, including photocopying, recording, taping or by any information storage retrieval system without the written permission of the publisher except in the case of brief quotations embodied in critical articles and reviews.

WestBow Press books may be ordered through booksellers or by contacting:

WestBow Press
A Division of Thomas Nelson & Zondervan
1663 Liberty Drive
Bloomington, IN 47403
www.westbowpress.com
1 (866) 928-1240

Because of the dynamic nature of the Internet, any web addresses or links contained in this book may have changed since publication and may no longer be valid. The views expressed in this work are solely those of the author and do not necessarily reflect the views of the publisher, and the publisher hereby disclaims any responsibility for them.

Any people depicted in stock imagery provided by Thinkstock are models, and such images are being used for illustrative purposes only. Certain stock imagery © Thinkstock.

ISBN: 978-1-4908-6909-4 (sc)
ISBN: 978-1-4908-6911-7 (hc)
ISBN: 978-1-4908-6910-0 (e)

Library of Congress Control Number: 2015901936

Print information available on the last page.

WestBow Press rev. date: 2/24/2015

CONTENTS

CHAPTER 1	The Announcement	1
CHAPTER 2	Business Begins	11
CHAPTER 3	Stepping Into Adulthood	17
CHAPTER 4	The Dirty Truth	23
CHAPTER 5	Downward Spiral	31
CHAPTER 6	Making Some Progress	36
CHAPTER 7	Reality Checks	41
CHAPTER 8	The Robbery	46
CHAPTER 9	Healing Begins	50
CHAPTER 10	Christmas Eve	57
CHAPTER 11	The Offer	63
CHAPTER 12	Checking It Out	68
CHAPTER 13	Parting Ways	74
CHAPTER 14	Bright New Beginnings	78
CHAPTER 15	Reality Hits Home	81
CHAPTER 16	Blood Guilt	85
CHAPTER 17	Unhappy Adventure	87
CHAPTER 18	It's a Boy!	93
CHAPTER 19	The Accident	98
CHAPTER 20	The Funeral	104
CHAPTER 21	The Visit	110
CHAPTER 22	The Wedding Day	117
CHAPTER 23	A Better Life	123

ACKNOWLEDGEMENTS

My sincerest thanks go to all my friends who supported, prayed for and encouraged me with this endeavor. My greatest thanks go to my four greatest supporters: my mother, Mary Boucot; and my three friends, Joan and Barb, who are avid readers and great encouragers; and MaryAnn who is an experienced business document editor.

I also want to thank my writer friends, Lori Boni, Robert Castle, and Edward Giambalvo from the Flemington Writers Meetup, who I have the privilege of meeting with every other Tuesday in the customer lounge at Boni Tire & Auto Service in Flemington, NJ. They have been a great source of excellent feedback on my work, providing information on resources, and giving me encouragement.

Thank you to all for your encouragement and support.

INTRODUCTION

Although this story takes place in a town that actually exists in southern New Jersey, the story is completely fictional. Some of the circumstances are realistic, but they are not real, and they are not real people. Even the layout of the streets and the town have been altered for the sake of this fictional story. However, many people have found themselves in similar circumstances in real life. So I'm sure that readers of this book will be able to relate to the people and the circumstances of this story. And I hope it touches people's hearts.

The only thing that is not completely realistic about the characters in this book is the language they use. Please understand that their language has been cleaned up considerably, especially since the bar scene and the people who frequent such places use profanity and vulgarity on a regular basis. I did this so that parents would not need to feel concerned if their children should pick up this book and read it and so that people who find such language offensive would not be offended in reading this story.

The book is about three young adults who start out their lives on shaky footing and come from home environments that are less than ideal. As a result of life crisis that each individual experiences, they each make choices to turn their lives around for the better and rise above the situations they grew up in.

I hope that this story about these three young people and the choices they make to take a better stand in their lives is an encouragement to the readers to make better choices to for their own lives.

Jesus said, "I am the way. . ." *John 14:6*

CHAPTER I

The Announcement

Judy watched mesmerized as an overwhelmingly large flock of blackbirds filled the sky and swooped across the field like a swarm of bees. All the while, her sister, Marge, was talking to her, and her last words were, "I guess you have no other place to go. You'll have to stay here."

"Huh, yeah," Judy said half-heartedly, tuning back into the conversation. She seemed more interested in the blackbirds than in the realities that lay ahead of her.

Marge was obviously annoyed and decided to throw some biting words out to rope Judy back to reality. "How did you get pregnant anyway?"

Judy smartly retorted, "How do you think?"

The attitude was unacceptable. Marge grabbed Judy's arm and swung her around to face her. "Now you listen to me. This is my home, and you're not going to treat me the way you treated Mom! You're sixteen years old. You're not working, and you need me more than I need you."

Judy always was a difficult kid, a classic case of a strong-willed child. When she lived at home, the battles were constant in trying to keep her under control and out of trouble. From looking at her, one would find this hard to believe because she gave the appearance of a perfect angel with her beautiful features, plus her long, straight blond hair and large soft brown eyes with long, thick lashes that flirtingly protruded from her silhouette. Yet, even the most saintly of parents would be put to the test by her vexing ways and fresh remarks. Marge, however, seemed determined that she was going to succeed where her mother failed.

In contrast to Judy, Marge looked much more like the Brennan side of the family, with strong but pretty features and soft, dark, bobbing curls that almost touched her shoulders. Her sparkling blue eyes were rimmed with dark lashes, and her face was covered with freckles. There was no mistaking that she was of Irish descent.

With great determination, Marge continued her conversation. "If you weren't so busy trying to be cool and tough and acting like a spoiled brat, maybe Mom wouldn't have told you to leave." However, it became obvious that arguing with her pregnant sister wasn't accomplishing much. So Marge composed herself and softened her approach. "Look, I never had any kids, and I've never been pregnant, but I would think being pregnant and working to support yourself would be very hard on you and the baby. So I don't expect you to get a job. In fact, I hope you don't. But you'll have to be responsible and apply for welfare or something to help out with household expenses. You'll also need to get state aid for paying your medical bills. There's no way that I would be able to pay for any of that."

The reality of living expenses and medical bills grabbed Judy's attention. "Oh, wow! Marge, I haven't even thought about that stuff yet. You know what? You are the best sister I could possibly ask for. I promise you, I'm really going to try hard to be responsible and be a good mom." With this, they both hugged as tears rimmed their eyes.

The year was 1973. Judy and Marge's father had died a couple of years before from a heart attack, leaving Mrs. Brennan alone with two daughters. It was only a week after Mr. Brennan died when Mrs. Brennan had a new boyfriend. She wasn't really looking for one, but it didn't take long for him to make his interest known. His name was Bill Bach, and he was the next-door neighbor who happened to be a widower for quite a few years previous to Joe Brennan's passing. Bill always said how he thought so very highly of Carla Brennan. He always said she was a tower of example. In truth, she was! Life with her husband, who was a heavy drinker, was not easy. But she steadfastly maintained a good attitude and lived her life as honorably as she could with her difficult circumstances.

Regardless of her mother's honorable character, Marge had a hard time accepting her mother's seeming frivolity and Bill's seeming to impetuously be *making a move*, as Marge put it, on her mother. So shortly after Bill started coming around, Marge moved out of the house and into a little cottage on the edge of a cornfield. It was an old, very small farmhand's cabin that happened to get rented out to whoever might be interested in living in such a remote little place. Her new neighborhood was a small cluster of similar farmhand's houses just off a rather rural county highway and just a little bit outside of town.

No one else blamed Carla Brennan for not grieving over her husband or for taking up so soon after with Bill because Joe Brennan wasn't such a great husband. One might have thought that since he always worked and brought home enough money to pay the bills, he must have been a reasonably good husband. However, with all the problems that came with his drinking and his great love for socializing at Custer's Bar and Grill, life with him was terribly unpleasant. When he wasn't working, he could usually be found at the bar. When he did finally come home, he was miserable and useless. Life for Carla was very difficult and lonely. And none of the work at home got done unless she did it. Amazingly, she never mentioned all the times he staggered in the door and passed out on the floor. Nor did she mention all the times he verbally berated her within hearing of the whole neighborhood. But these kinds of things happened regularly.

As far as Judy went, no one could be completely sure if Mr. Brennan's lifestyle affected Judy's behavior or if Judy was such a difficult child because she was just naturally strong-willed. In either case, Judy's growing up years only served to compound the difficulties in her mother's life. And the older Judy got, the worse the types of trouble she got into had become.

"Judy," Marge continued the conversation, "I'm hoping you *really* understand what it means to be responsible and what it takes to be a good mother. You know this will mean that you've got to stop messing with the drugs and the booze, and you've got to stay out of trouble with the guys. You've got to stop being a kid and running all around town with your friends. You'll also have to go to bed at a reasonable time. And you'll have to take care of yourself and your baby. Plus, you'll have to pay bills, do some housework, and keep up your end of the household as much as possible. I'm afraid that being responsible for yourself and your baby is going to mean a lot of big changes for you."

Judy just looked at Marge with eyes opened wide in wonder about the consequences she was about to face for the things she had done.

"Who is the father, anyway?"

Judy looked away from Marge's stern gaze in shame. Contemplating the tremendous changes and responsibilities this baby would bring into her life, she gave a dazed reply: "Dan Schisler."

"Dan Schisler! I know him. I know his dad too. They are both customers of mine at the bar. Wow!"

In 1973, the drinking age was lowered to eighteen in New Jersey. So, twenty-year-old Danny was permitted by law to drink at the bar.

Buddy Custer, who was the owner of Custer's Bar and Grill, gave Marge a job as a barmaid when she was just barely twenty-one. Traditionally, Buddy only hired older men because sometimes the place got pretty rough. However, Mr. Brennan was a good customer of his, and Buddy knew Marge was a pretty tough and sensible young woman. When he found out Marge needed a better paying job because she had moved out on her own, and she was struggling to get by with the money she made at the deli, he offered her a daytime barmaid position that she gratefully accepted. It was well known that bar help at Custer's made excellent tip money because it was a very busy bar and a good portion of the customers made decent wages.

"Well, what do you think of him?" Judy asked, wrinkling her brow in uncertainty. "He's twenty, just a few years younger than you, and he has a good job."

"Does he know you're pregnant?"

"No."

Marge cocked her head with disdain. "Well, Judy, I doubt if he cares either!"

"How can you say that?"

"Listen, Judy, I'm not trying to be nasty, but I know that guy. He is a very likeable person, but he's not the caring, responsible kind. Not the family kind for certain! I don't think you know what you've gotten yourself into."

"You've got to give him a chance!" Judy pleaded.

"Well, okay. We'll give him a chance. I think you should talk to him as soon as possible and see what he plans to do."

The following morning, Judy was sipping her tea, dreaming about her, Danny, and the baby as a happy little family. Marge was already at work. Buddy would only give her day hours during the week when things were a little quieter and when businessmen and construction workers would come in for lunch. With the daytime clientele, there usually wasn't any rough behavior going on. Therefore, Marge was blessed with working Monday through Friday from 8:00 a.m. to 4:00 p.m. Since Judy was left alone, she had a whole day to think and dream. She thought about names and pondered whether she wanted a boy or a girl. She decided to postpone anything to do with getting welfare money or anything like that. Marge had to be wrong. Danny would make a good father and husband. He would certainly marry her and spare her the shame of being an unwed mother—and spare his baby the hardship of being an illegitimate child.

Early that evening, she called him. It was the best time to call because he would be just finishing his dinner after working all day.

"Hi, Danny! It's Judy."

"Hi, sweetheart! What's up?" Judy didn't realize it, but Danny called all the girls *sweetheart*.

"I was just wondering what you were doing because I'd like to see you."

"Well, I guess I'll be over in just a little bit. I will need to freshen up first."

"I'm not at my mom's. I'm at my sister Marge's." She gave him the directions how to get there. Then afterward, she proceeded to make herself pretty for him.

After she hung up, she hollered, "Marge, Danny is coming over in just a little bit. Please let us talk alone, okay?"

"Sure, no problem," Marge replied from her bedroom.

Judy planned to walk out in back of the cottage into the cornfield with Danny. It was quiet and romantic—and perhaps the right atmosphere to make him agreeable to the news she was about to disclose to him.

A short while later, a shiny new, fully dressed Harley pulled up on the front lawn. A tall, wiry-built Danny lifted his helmet to reveal dark, thick, shoulder-length hair and one gleaming gold earring in his left ear. In those days, chopped Harleys were considered really cool. Flower power was no longer the *in* thing. Guys who were really cool went around looking like some type of degenerate—a Hell's Angel or a retired hippie. Danny, however, had a style of his own. He did like his hair long, and he did like his earring. But he always looked neatly dressed and clean. His brand new, unchopped Harley was always polished. He made it clear to everyone that he liked his image because it seemed to make everyone happy. He looked good enough to please his neighbors or to go to work. And his peers found his style trendy enough to be acceptable. Plus, he was flashy enough to impress the girls. He definitely wasn't shy.

A flushed Judy was patting her face to keep it from burning. The doorbell rang, and she flew to answer it.

"Hi, sweetheart!" Dan grinned. Then he saw Marge. "Hi, Marge!" giving his biggest, most winsome smile.

"Hi," Marge said sharply as she turned and walked away.

"We're going for a walk, Marge," Judy said as she shut the door behind her.

"Nice place your sister has! This is my style. Out of the way but not too far out."

"Yeah! Cheap too!" Pausing with embarrassment, Judy corrected herself, "I mean it's not expensive."

When they cleared the corner of the cornfield, Danny held her close and placed his hands on the small of her back. She felt as if she could have melted. He wasn't especially handsome, but he really knew how to charm a girl.

"Danny, I've got to talk to you!" She pulled herself away from his grasp.

"Oh yeah?" He gave her a puzzled look.

"Have you ever been married before?"

"Are you proposing to me?" he asked with a raised eyebrow.

"No!" Uncertain how to continue, Judy wrinkled her brow.

"You're pregnant!" was Danny's next conclusion.

Judy's relieved sigh gave Danny his answer.

"I don't believe it! You're pregnant, and you want me to marry you. Is that it?" Danny stood with both hands on his hips and his head cocked, looking at Judy incredulously.

Embarrassed, Judy looked away, "I don't know what I want."

"Have you considered getting rid of it?"

"You mean abortion?" Judy looked horrified at Danny.

"Yeah, abortion!"

"It's not legal!" Judy whined.

"Well, we'll find someone to do it illegally!" Danny swung one hand in the air as if the solution would be that simple.

"No, Danny!" Judy appeared surprised with herself for saying no to this guy whom she loved and dreamed about so much. "First of all, how do I know this person doing the abortion wouldn't make a mistake and kill me too? After all, I hear so many stories about girls getting hurt in illegal abortions. Second of all, I don't want any dead babies on my conscience."

Danny's next easy fix was, "All right! How about putting the baby up for adoption?"

"If I'm going to have my baby, I'm going to keep it. It's my child!" Judy started crying. "It's your baby too. Don't you care? So maybe you wouldn't be interested in me, but aren't you at least interested in your own baby? Don't you want to give the baby your name?"

Danny just put his hands in his pockets and gave her a blank, disbelieving look. Judy got the message. He wasn't interested in her or his own baby. She let out the most bitter sob and ran back to the cottage.

As she bolted into the kitchen crying, Marge tried to catch her to hug and console her, but she broke free to go collapse on the sofa. She watched from the window sobbing bitterly as Danny stormed to his bike swearing and making hostile expressions and gestures.

Marge sat on the sofa beside Judy and put her hands on her shoulders. In a soft tone of voice, Marge tried to comfort her. "I don't want to say anything to upset you, but I expected him to act this way, and you're probably better off. Let him go. You and the baby will be better off."

Judy was quiet for a few minutes. Then she broke out sobbing again, "How do you feel about having an unwed mother and an illegitimate child living with you?"

Marge lovingly embraced her. "I had an idea it would be like this when you first told me. I know it's not the best way to start off in life, but it'll be okay. You and the baby will survive. Besides that, I think it'll be neat being an aunt. And I think we'll all be just fine."

But Judy was inconsolable. She just cried the better part of the night. The next morning, Marge came out from her bedroom and found Judy asleep on the sofa with an empty tissue box and used tissues in a big pile on the floor.

"Judy, maybe you should sleep in your bed," Marge said as she gently nudged her and picked up the pile of tissues.

The cottage was very small but just adequate for the two girls to be comfortable. The furnishings were very modest. All of it was either donated or Marge purchased it from the Salvation Army. The front door opened into a large room that was a combined living room and kitchen, with the kitchen area to the left. In the middle of the back wall were three doors clustered together. From right to left, the first door was to Marge's bedroom; the second was to a very small bathroom; the third was to a pantry or storage type of room that Marge made into a guest room since she didn't really have much to store. So naturally, the guest room now became Judy's bedroom. Then there was another door going outside from the kitchen area.

Judy didn't seem to move much at all after Marge nudged her. So after putting all the tissues in the trash, Marge walked back over and nudged her again. "Maybe you should go to bed."

Rubbing the sleep from swollen eyes, Judy shook her head no.

"Well then, come talk to me." Marge motioned her to sit at the kitchen table. "So what did he say anyway?"

Judy obligingly got up to join her. "Well, first he asked if I considered getting rid of the baby. Then he asked if I considered finding a family to adopt the baby. I don't know, Marge. This whole thing was a big mistake. Why did I have to get pregnant? I knew it was wrong. Mom always taught us that the right way to do things was to get married first. She's right, and I shouldn't have argued with her so bad about the whole thing."

"All right, stop beating yourself up. It's not going to help the situation. So tell me what happened next when you and Danny were out back?"

"I burst out crying and ran to the house, and I guess he went home."

"Uh-huh." Marge started water boiling for tea and cooking some eggs in the frying pan. "Well, how do you feel about these options?"

"Well, I sure can't put my own baby up for adoption, and I don't know about abortion." Without a pause, Judy continued, "And why are you frying those eggs? You never eat breakfast."

"I know. These eggs are for you. You need nourishment in your condition."

Judy giggled. "Marge, you really mean what you said about it being okay that I'm going to be an unwed mother with an illegitimate baby? Do you really mind being an aunt and having me live here under these conditions?"

"You've got to pick up the pieces and go from here. And I really don't want to sway your decisions one way or the other."

"Yeah. Sure, Marge. That's why you're frying those eggs," Judy chided.

Marge laughed. "Look, Judy. Would you really want to have an abortion? You have a real live baby in your belly. Besides that, abortion is illegal. Where would you go to get it done? Who? What kind of person would be doing this procedure? And how could you not love your own baby, even if this is not the right way to go about things?"

Judy sighed. "You know, Marge, I really hate myself for being so stupid. I wasn't even thinking about what I was getting myself into, and now I've ruined two lives, mine and the baby's. And no one cares—not Mom, not Danny. Just you!"

"Look. Let's not get so dramatic," Marge said as she placed the eggs, salt, and pepper in front of Judy. "Other girls have illegitimate babies, and things work out all right for them. They even marry after it's all over. As I said before, it's not the best way to do things, but it doesn't have to be the end of the world either."

"Well, you gave me the eggs. Where's my knife and fork?" Judy smiled.

Marge chuckled as she gave Judy her utensils. "Good! Keep smiling! You don't want to get my niece or nephew upset."

"You really think I should keep the baby, don't you?" Judy paused with amusement. "There really is a baby in there! I guess it would be nice to have a baby," she said as she rubbed her hand over her belly. Then worry set in. "What if the welfare office wants to know who the father is? Should I tell them?"

"Hmm-m-m!" Marge's eyebrows went up as she thought a few seconds. "Well, if they try to keep your money from you until you tell them, I would. But if you do tell them, he might demand rights to see his kid and make a pain out of himself. Would you want him coming around? You'll have to think about it and decide for yourself." With that said, Marge headed to her bedroom with her traditional cup of instant coffee to get dressed for work.

Judy looked undecided as she thought to herself, *Maybe he would change his mind when he sees his baby.*

"I just thought of something," Marge shouted out to Judy. "Will you be going to school now that you're pregnant?"

"No way! I can't face all those kids at school knowing they will eventually find out that I'm pregnant. I would not be able to finish out the school year anyway. That would be just plain humiliating! I just can't do that!"

Marge was standing in her bedroom door as she waited to see what Judy's response would be. "You know we'll have to tell the school. We need to talk about this before I leave for work. I'll be back out in a minute."

Judy quietly remembered how charming Danny was before he rejected her and the baby. Then anger shot through her. "I could puke," she mumbled to herself, "or is it morning sickness?" The more she thought about it, the more she could see no benefit in revealing the father's name and hoped the people at the welfare office would not make an issue about it. Whatever happened, Judy resolved to herself that she was going to show everyone she could handle all the responsibilities of pregnancy and motherhood like a mature adult. She was going to make good for all her mistakes.

Breezing back into the kitchen, Marge was almost ready to leave for work. "Now tell me, do you want me to call the school for you?"

"I can't talk to the school about my being pregnant! It's just too embarrassing," Judy answered. It was amazing how quickly her resolve had begun to diminish.

"All right. I'll call them from work today and see what they want us to do. Bye!" Marge said as she hurriedly headed for the kitchen door.

Judy stopped her. "What would you like me to do for dinner?"

"Be creative. You'll have to be," Marge laughed. "There isn't much selection until I go shopping."

"Yeah, okay! Bye," Judy chuckled.

CHAPTER 2

Business Begins

Custer's Bar and Grill was about two blocks into the business district of Woodbury if coming from the direction of Marge's house. She always found it hard to believe that people would start drinking so early in the morning. Some of the people may have actually been doing business. But most of them were just the old-timers starting out their day socializing with a few drinks. *Amazing!* she would say to herself. *How can people drink so early in the morning?*

Most of the daytime customers were pretty nice. The group, that Buddy would chidingly call the *old-timers*, was a small group of old retired men that met regularly at Custer's just to hang out. Most of the time, they truly were lovable. However, once in a while, one of them would get a load on and become unbearable.

They all loved Margie, and they each told her so often during the day, especially Jesse. Each time one of them would say they loved her, she would roll her eyes up to the ceiling. At first impression, Marge appeared to be a snob with a slightly turned up nose and a cool nature. However, her enthusiasm in her work and her friendly, sparkling nature soon warmed the hearts of all who met her.

"Marge, I've got a beer order coming in at the basement," said Buddy as he headed to the basement steps. "That's where I'll be until about lunchtime. If you need me, holler down from the kitchen door like you usually do. Okay?"

"Okay," she said. "But sometime today I've got to make a phone call to my sister's school, and it might take a few minutes. When you have a few free minutes to take over, would you let me know, so I can go make my call?"

Buddy stopped in his tracks with interest. "Sure. But I'm curious ... why are you calling for her?"

Marge stepped over close to Buddy and quietly told him the whole story so the customers at the bar could not hear what she was saying.

"Oh my!" Buddy commented. He was a sweet and quiet man who sometimes seemed rather passive. But in reality, he was just a very peace-loving person who was trying to be non-offensive. "I'll make sure I come back up before lunch so you can get your call done before the lunch rush comes in. You know how busy it gets. It's much better if we're both behind the bar when the lunch crowd gets here."

"Thanks, Buddy!"

"Oh, Miss Margie." Jesse Golden signaled with his empty glass, "Did I tell you I love you today?"

"What a character!" Marge commented to Buddy as she went to refill Jesse's glass.

The bar itself was horseshoe shaped, with the cash register, the entrance to the bar, and the entrance to the kitchen all at the front right corner of the horseshoe. The length of the bar was roughly thirty feet all the way around. Walking in from the entrance to the bar room, the first thing one would see was the cash register. To the left and along the next two walls were tables and chairs. And between the far wall and the bar was a large open area with a nine-foot pool table.

The tables and chairs seldom got used except during lunchtime. Custer's packed the customers in at lunchtime. Every table and bar stool would be taken. Then after lunch was over, most of the customers would go back to work, but there were always a few who would stay at the bar until evening. Since Buddy had Marge working for him during the day, business picked up quite a bit. It seemed that having a pretty young woman behind the bar attracted more business.

Buddy finally finished stacking, checking, rotating the beer, and then mopping, cleaning, and organizing the basement. This was his usual Thursday routine. "Okay, Marge, go make your call. I'll take over now. Just be quick because the lunch crowd should be coming in soon."

"You mean you aren't serving us anymore?" Arnie called out to Marge. "You know how much we love you!"

Marge rolled her eyes to the ceiling, "Yeah, Arnie. Don't worry. I'll be right back. I just have a phone call to make."

She went into the kitchen to use the business phone. There she got the school's number from information and then made her call. "Hi! I'm Marge Brennan. I'm calling for my sister. I think I should talk to the principal. Can I speak to him?"

The woman on the other end of the call told Marge that she would see if Mr. Dumont could come to the phone.

After waiting a minute or two, he picked up the phone. "Hello, this is George Dumont. How can I help you?"

"Hello, Mr. Dumont. This is Marge Brennan. I'm calling for my sister, Judy Brennan. I don't know how to say this, but she is pregnant, and I'm sure she would not be able to finish out this school year. She's due to deliver in May, and she's a junior in your school right now."

Mr. Dumont quietly gasped and then quickly composed himself, "Well, Miss Brennan, I'm sorry to hear all this. Does your mother know?"

"Yes," Marge stated uncomfortably, "but Judy is living with me. So that shouldn't matter, right?"

"Quite contrary, Miss Brennan. You said she's a junior. How old is she?"

"Sixteen!" Marge frowned with a worried look.

"Yes, I was afraid of that. You see, when a child is sixteen years old or under, they're still considered a minor. In fact, she legally cannot really claim responsibility for herself until she is eighteen."

"I thought that at sixteen she could just drop out of school."

"At sixteen, she can drop out of school, but she still needs parental consent. I'm afraid that being sixteen does not make one emancipated in the eyes of the law. You said your mother knows already. So why should you be concerned? Your mother really does know, doesn't she?"

"Yes, but there has been some hard feelings between her and Judy." That was only part of the truth. The other part of the truth was Marge did not want her mother to take away the credit for helping Judy through this difficult situation. Secretly, Marge wanted to be able to rub it in to her mother later on that they didn't need her. She wanted to be able to say that she could handle situations much better than her mother.

"According to the laws regarding compulsory education, all children between the ages of six and sixteen are required to attend school. As I said before, a child can only drop out of school at age sixteen with parental consent. I'm afraid only your mother has the authority to come in and sign the forms giving consent for Judy to drop out of school."

"All right. I guess I'll call Mom and see what she will do."

"Very good, Miss Brennan." Mr. Dumont tried to sound as consoling and reassuring as possible. "I hope to hear from your mother in the next day or so. You certainly would not want to have truancy problems on your hands. In the meantime, school counseling and tutoring for Judy to work on her GED are available if she would like."

"Okay, I'll let her know. Thanks, Mr. Dumont. We'll get back to you. Good-bye." Marge replied and then hung up the phone. *Oh, swell*, she said to herself as she rubbed her face in despair. Turning around, she leaned her back up against the kitchen counter. She crossed her arms and looked down at the floor, wondering what would happen if she just didn't bother to straighten things out with the school. *Oh no! I can't do that. The truant officer would be at my door making trouble now that the principal knows where she's at.*

Marge had a real dilemma because even though she didn't want any trouble with the school, and she genuinely wanted to help her sister, she wanted as little to do with her mother as possible. Marge struggled with herself because of the bitterness she harbored against her mother about Bill Bach and all those difficult years growing up with a father who drank so much. Marge always felt her mother was too much of a doormat with both her father and with Judy. She wanted to show her mother how to stand up to people and how to take control of life and situations. Now, instead, she was going to have to go to her mother for help. Marge felt quite uncomfortable with calling her, but she braced herself to make the call because she knew this needed to be done.

So she got right back on the phone and called her mother. "Hi, Mom. It's Margie."

Mrs. Brennan paused and then sweetly answered, "Hello, Margie! It's so good to hear from you."

"I guess you know Judy came to stay with me," Marge said, feeling her mother out.

"I figured she would, and I'm glad you called. Does she know you're calling me?"

"Not yet!" Marge shifted her weight from one foot to the other wondering how she should approach her mother. "You know Judy is pregnant, right?"

"Yes, I do. The news of her pregnancy was part of what precipitated the big argument we had when I told her she had to leave."

Now Marge was ready to relay the message from Mr. Dumont. "Well,

Judy wants to drop out of school now that she's pregnant. So I called the school today, and the principal, Mr. Dumont, said that in order for Judy to drop out of school, he would have to see you in person, and that you would have to sign a consent statement giving her the permission."

"Okay," her mother responded thoughtfully. "I'll go to the school tomorrow and take care of everything."

"Okay." Disappointment hung in Marge's face. "He said also something about counseling and tutoring for a GED. I haven't talked to her about it yet, but I have a feeling she won't be interested in any of that." Marge continued on, "You might like to know that I told her she would have to be responsible for herself, do some housework, get state aid, and pay her own bills. However, I'm not encouraging her to go to work. I think it's better for her to get rest for her and the baby."

"You're so right, Marge," her mother replied as amicably as possible. "I think you'll be a good influence on her. You're a good person, and you've always had good common sense. I've been hoping and praying that you will be able to help her to get her act together. You might be her last chance to straighten up her life before she really ruins it. Sometimes all a person needs is another chance. I've repeatedly told her she can't go carrying on in life like she did at home. That's why when she threatened to run away the last time, I told her to go. I thought and prayed about it ahead of time and decided that's what I had to do the next time she had one of her tantrums. There was really nothing else I could do with her." Her mother's voice became a little apologetic as she continued, "And I figured she would go to your house first, and I knew if she did, you would try to help her."

Marge was quite taken back by her mother's statement. "Well, I guess it was a good thing that I set down the house rules right from the start." Marge was a little distant. She was wondering if her mother was really smart enough to plan a strategy like that to make Judy straighten up. Marge was even more taken back by all her mother said about her being a good influence, and a good person, and having good common sense. She found her mother's favorable opinion of her to be unexpected and wondered how to respond.

In addition to that, what her mother just said resonated with a sound logic that did not fit in with what she remembered about her. Marge always used to think to herself, *Sure, Mom, you pray and quote Scripture at people, but anyone who acts that good when Dad comes home falling-down drunk, calling you all those filthy names and throwing things around, has got to be a dope.*

Marge used to think her mother used her faith as a crutch because she was too spineless to stand up otherwise. She certainly didn't impress Marge as someone who would have a strategy for handling Judy as she just said she did and then be strong enough to follow through with it.

"Marge, I don't want Judy to think I've softened. So, please don't tell her I offered. But if you need money or anything else, please call, okay?"

Marge was stunned as she blinked back tears. "Thanks, Mom. Right now, we're okay for money. But later on, I'm sure Judy will need baby things. Outside of that, I think we'll manage all right." She paused, and then quickly blurted out, "Oh yeah. I guess she'll need maternity clothes pretty soon."

"Okay, I'll look around the house and see what kind of loose clothing I can find. Can I drop them off to you at Custer's? This way Judy won't know where they came from."

"Sure. Thanks, Mom."

"Marge, I won't be coming into the bar. So I'll just leave them in your car, okay?"

"Okay, Mom." Marge knew her mother would not come into the bar because she did not approve of such places.

"I hope she doesn't make trouble for you," her mother stated in a concerned tone.

"Well, so far everything is going fine. I guess you would like me to keep you posted on how things are going."

"Please do, Marge. And make sure she keeps all her doctor appointments. Make sure she has a neighbor she can call on for help and rides while you're at work. And remember, 'God makes all things work out for the good.'"

"Okay," Marge said, chuckling to herself. She recognized the Scripture verse because of all the years of living with her mother quoting Scripture at her.

"Bye, Marge! I love you!" her mother's voice quivered.

"I love you too, Mom! Bye!"

Marge's mother sobbed quietly as she hung up the phone. Marge caught on to it. As she hung up the phone, she struggled a little with her own feelings as she thought to herself, *I guess Mom's been through a lot.* But within a few seconds, Marge was back into her business as usual form.

"Okay, Buddy, let the lunches begin. I'm back!"

CHAPTER 3

Stepping Into Adulthood

It was early October, when all of life was changing colors. While Marge was busy at work, Judy was also busy at home finding out what she could for getting state financial aid. She had no idea what an eye-opening experience she was about to embark upon. Responsibility was about to take on new substance for her.

On calling the local municipal office, she found out she would have to go to the welfare office in Woodbury to apply for welfare, food stamps, and Medicaid. This meant she would have to walk to the bus stop and take the bus into Woodbury. This was likely going to be an almost all-day ordeal.

The Gloucester County Welfare Department was spread out over the second floor of an old medical building on a corner on Broad Street. Woodbury, which was the closest city, better resembled a large town than a city. It was located in the flatlands of southern New Jersey, and the surrounding area was sort of rural. There were plenty of stores and other businesses along Broad Street, which happened to be the main street, and a few businesses and offices along some of the side streets. The whole business district of Woodbury was a little more than ten blocks long.

Judy nervously stepped off the bus in front of the building. Her stomach was churning. Some of this discomfort was because of the pregnancy, but some of it was because she was so intimidated by all the stories she heard about the legalities and paperwork ahead of her.

She followed the signs with arrows saying *Welfare Applicants* to the second floor. At the top of the second flight of steps, she saw a desk with a sign saying *Receptionist*. The woman seated at the desk appeared to be a sweet, motherly type in her fifties. She smiled at Judy and asked if she could help her. Judy told her she was there to apply for welfare. So the lady took Judy's name and directed her to the waiting room. Judy took a seat in one of the folding chairs lined up around the perimeter of the room. After sitting there a few minutes, she became aware of a peculiar odor. She realized it was the woman sitting two seats away. One would guess her to be in her late twenties or early thirties. She had medium length raggedy brown curls peeking out from a red cotton bandana. Her teeth were dark yellow from cigarette smoke. Her skin was leathery. Her clothes were worn and dirty looking.

She could be sort of attractive looking if she cleaned up and dressed better, Judy thought to herself. *After all, she's built okay, and she's not really ugly. I can't believe someone would let herself go like that. What a pig! There's really no excuse for that.*

Judy became very uncomfortable. She tried to look at anything but this woman. She didn't want to be rude, but the idea that this was the kind of person who was associated with welfare, and that she might be associated with someone like this, was disconcerting. This made Judy feel quite uncomfortable and embarrassed about applying for welfare.

There was another woman on the opposite side of the room. She was very clean and attractive, which gave Judy a feeling of relief. In the middle of the room were six young children ranging in age from toddler to about five years old. Two of them were black. Then one of the black children went up to the clean woman and called her *Mommy*. Then Judy realized the other four children bore a resemblance to the dirty looking woman and assumed they all belonged to her. Judy wondered who would ever get so close to such a dirty, smelly woman. Then it dawned on Judy the dirty woman was wearing a maternity blouse and was a few months pregnant. Judy's heart sank. She really didn't want to be associated with such a thing as this dirty woman.

Judy didn't even want to sit by her. She got up and pretended to be looking for something to read, just so she could change her seat.

Finally, a woman came into the room and called, "Judy Brennan." She followed the woman into the next room where the woman asked her a lot of questions and wrote in Judy's answers on the application form. Looking suspiciously at Judy, the woman fired one question after another. It seemed like the woman must have thought the welfare money belonged to her rather than the state that she was working for.

"Name? Social Security number? Date of birth? How old are you? Where do you live? Do you live with your parents or other family members? Do you own your home? Do you pay rent? Are you supported by anyone else? Do you have any bank accounts? Do you have any life insurance? Do you have any stocks or bonds? Do you own a car? Do you have any other valuables worth mentioning?"

The experience of making the application and answering the questions was unsettling enough, but the most difficult was yet to come. "Who is the father?"

Judy paused. She didn't want to seem like some lowlife who just slept around like that dirty woman in the waiting room who didn't know who the father was. But she didn't want to tell the interviewer Danny's name either. She was so hurt by him that she just wanted as little to do with him as possible.

"You know who the father is, don't you?" the interviewer asked with one eyebrow raised.

Judy wondered if this woman knew anyone that she could gossip to about her. She decided she would rather fight with Danny than face that humiliation. "Danny Schisler," she mumbled.

The interviewer's other eyebrow went up to match the first eyebrow, as she filled in the answer. "His address?"

Judy was distracted, wondering if this snotty interviewer knew Danny.

"His address?" the interviewer repeated.

Nervously, Judy gave part of his address to her and pretended that she didn't know his full address.

The interviewer wrote down what information Judy was willing to give her, and then flatly stated, "Okay! Sign here! That's all for today."

As Judy signed the application, she asked "Do I get a check today?"

The woman pursed her lips and then told Judy that she would get her evaluation notice or her first check in the mail in thirty days.

"Thirty days! Wow!" Judy moaned. "What if I was starving to death and really desperate for money?"

"Are you?" the snotty interviewer quipped.

"Well, I'm not starving to death, but I do need the money." Then Judy's feisty side surfaced in retaliation. "But what if I was starving to death?"

The interviewer snippily replied, "Then you can go down the hall and apply for food stamps."

"Oh, okay. Thanks. Would I be able to get them right away?"

"No," the interviewer said curtly. "You will know if you're approved for the food stamps pretty much right away. But you would have to wait for two weeks for them to arrive in your mail."

Still feeling argumentative, Judy replied, "Well, what if I can't wait that long?"

"Then you would have to go to a food pantry, a church, Salvation Army, or something like that." The interviewer's voice escalated to plain orneriness, "But it doesn't appear that you're starving to death. So there's no sense in getting upset about it, is there?"

"No, I guess not," Judy backed away from the interviewer's desk and put all her papers into her purse. Feeling terribly humiliated, she turned to leave the room.

"Have a nice day!" the interviewer sneered at Judy as she walked out the door.

Judy could feel tears escaping from the corners of her eyes as she headed back through the waiting room to the receptionist desk. She restrained herself from having a dramatic outburst and just quietly muttered every filthy name she could think of under her breath. She was glad she decided to restrain herself. After all, that interviewer could make some real trouble for her. Then she wondered if that interviewer would be mean enough to lose her application papers or something like that.

Just as Judy was about to slip through the door leading to the steps, the receptionist, realizing Judy was distressed, jumped up from her seat just in time to catch Judy by the arm.

"Are you okay, honey?"

"That interview was awful. And the woman who interviewed me was so nasty."

The receptionist looked around as if to see who might be listening. "Oh, I know who you mean. Don't worry about her. She doesn't get along well with anyone. Not even the people she works with."

"Do you think she would lose my application or get me rejected from getting welfare?"

The receptionist reassured her, "That's not her decision! All applications are handled by standard procedure, and if anyone gets caught tampering with government papers, they'll find themselves in big trouble. I'm sure she wants to keep her job. So she wouldn't do any such thing."

Then the receptionist walked Judy by the hand over to the seat next to her desk to chat some more. She reminded Judy of her mother because she was so gentle, warm, and caring. She brought some tissues and a paper cup full of water from the water cooler to Judy and continued, "Before you head home, sit down and calm down some." Judy gratefully took the tissues and water. And before long, she found herself telling the woman her whole life story about getting pregnant, getting into an argument with her mother, and moving in with her sister. Judy wasn't sure if this woman really cared as much as she seemed to, but she was glad to have a listening ear. She went on to tell her about how Danny didn't seem to care, and then she stopped abruptly to ask the receptionist, "Do you think they will contact Danny?"

"Well, if you told the interviewer he's the father, they will probably try to make him pay."

"Oh swell! Then he'll be at my door giving me trouble for ratting on him."

"They'll have to prove he's the father, and that's not easy to do. If I were you, I wouldn't spend too much energy worrying about that. You have more important things to think about."

Judy felt like she knew this woman all her life, and she seemed to be the only one who cared besides Marge. Every time she came back to the welfare office after this incident, she would have to stop to talk to Ronnie. Her real name was Veronica, but she insisted Judy call her Ronnie.

"How could they prove Danny was the father?" Judy asked.

"The best evidence is a blood test, and the blood test isn't always that reliable. It works by process of elimination, so it still isn't really conclusive enough evidence to make him responsible. Also, he could get a lawyer and contest it."

Ronnie's words were very comforting to Judy. She thought to herself, maybe her mother was right about how God puts the right people in the right place at the right time.

Suddenly Judy remembered that maybe she should do her application for the food stamps. So she changed the conversation. "I didn't realize I would have to put in another application for food stamps. Can you tell me where I would go for that?"

Ronnie directed her to go down the steps and then turn to the hall on the right.

"Ronnie, thank you so much for being so nice to me. I really appreciate it." Judy stood up and caught herself as she almost kissed Ronnie good-bye. Then she acted as if she just lost her balance a little.

Ronnie pretended nothing happened and smiled sweetly as she said "Bye, dear!" As she watched Judy head down the steps, she sighed to herself, "Lord, what a shame! Please help that girl get her life back on track. Please talk to the baby's father and make him see what a big mistake it would be to abandon his child like that." Then she sympathetically shook her head as she went back to her work.

CHAPTER 4

The Dirty Truth

It was 4:00 p.m. on a Friday, and Marge just finished wiping the bar down when she decided to have a couple of drinks before heading home. Custer's employees were allowed to have a few drinks on the premises as long as they didn't make any trouble or drink during their work hours. She usually never stayed late because she didn't like to be there if any fights broke out. Local people sometimes called Custer's Bar and Grill *Custer's Last Stand* because there was at least one good bar fight a week in there.

Marge was busy gazing out the windows at the flamboyant colors of the few nearby trees in town when she noticed Danny Schisler coming in through the door at the far side of the bar over by the pool table. Since most bar pool tables were pay tables, and each game cost a quarter, it became a convenient bar custom in all the local bars to line up quarters as a way of keeping track of which person was playing the next game. So Danny put his quarter in line with the two quarters already lined up on the edge of the table. Then he went to the bar and said hello to a few of his friends. Then he placed his cigarette on the edge of the ashtray as he pulled money from his wallet and ordered his beer. Once his beer arrived, he took one sip. Then he looked up and noticed Marge, who had not taken her eyes off him since he walked into the bar.

"Gerry, would you move my drink to the other side of the bar?" Danny picked up his cigarettes and all his money, and asked one of his friends to let him know when his quarter was up next.

Gerry Blazeuski was the bartender for the weekend nights. The customers sometimes called him *Bluto*. He earned the nickname by his tremendous build and great strength. He was divorced and working two jobs because he had to pay alimony and child support for two children. His friends wondered how he found the time, but in his spare time he lifted weights. His neck was almost bigger around than his head. Potential troublemakers would tremble just looking at him. In reality, he really was a very likeable guy and not as fearsome as he might appear. Buddy may have hired him for the weekend nights just for his physical appearance.

As soon as Marge realized Danny was coming around the bar to sit next to her, she turned her face away and leaned her head on her hand.

"Hi, Marge! I guess you know the whole story about me and Judy."

"What story?" she sarcastically replied.

"Come on, Marge! Don't play games with me. I just wanted to talk to you. I feel really bad about the whole thing."

Marge didn't say a word. She just let him keep talking as she sipped her rum and Coke and looked around.

Danny continued on, "If she would get rid of it or find a home for the kid, I would be glad to pay the expenses."

Still silence.

Danny looked down as he said, "I'm sorry. I'm just not ready to be a father right now."

After taking a big gulp of her drink, she flashed him a cold look. "I'll relay the message when I get home. Now buzz off!"

"Okay! Okay!" Danny got the message. He was not going to justify himself to Marge. And he wasn't going to make trouble as long as Gerry was there. He walked back around the bar to the pool table.

"What happened? Did she turn you down?" Freddie Deitz laughingly bellowed at him. Freddie and Danny were good friends.

"I wasn't asking her out," chuckled Danny. "What turn am I?"

"There's one quarter before you," Fred answered.

Danny was a frequent visitor at Custer's because he not only liked to socialize and drink, but he liked to play pool. The pool table at Custer's was one of the best bar tables in the area. By looking at it, one would never know how good it really was because there were a few stains on the felt and it was just a common nine-foot slate barroom table. But the table was perfectly level and straight, and there was plenty of room all around the table to make shots without worrying about the back of the cue stick banging a wall or a support post. When the balls rolled, there was never a deviation in how they rolled ... no curves, no slants, perfect!

Oh, yes. Dan had one other reason for frequenting Custer's. That was to meet girls. There wasn't much entertainment in the area, and this was a generation that did not have quite as much reservation about women being in bars as previous generations. He rarely went out on dates with girls because he could flirt all he wanted at the bar with no strings attached and very little money spent, except what he might spend on 2:00 a.m. breakfast at the diner after Custer's was closed. If he did buy a girl breakfast, he of course expected to go to bed with her right after.

After Danny settled back down on the pool side of the bar, Gerry leaned over to the bar to comment to Marge, "I don't blame you. You got good taste to get rid of that scumbag."

Marge giggled at Gerry's comment and leaned over to tell him, "Oh, if you only knew. There's more to it than that."

"Yeah?" Gerry raised an eyebrow and waited for her to go on.

Looking around behind her to see if anyone was within earshot, Marge proceeded to tell Gerry the story about Danny and Judy.

Gerry heaved a sigh. "Someday he's going to get himself in real trouble. Then he will be sorry!"

The sink station set up for washing and storing the bar glasses was to Marge's left just behind the bar. Gerry washed a few dirty glasses and came back to Marge. "I don't know how Danny does it. Jesse and Art were in here late one day last weekend, and we got to talking. They said he works a full-time job during the day with his dad. And yet, I know this guy stays out until three o'clock in the morning and later almost every night. I go to the gym three or four night a week, and work a full-time job, and this part-time job. And if I don't get at least six hours sleep a night, it catches up with me." Shaking his head in disbelief, he went on, "He can't be getting more than three or four hours of sleep most nights, and maybe even less if he takes a girl to breakfast and does you know what later."

Gerry served a few drinks and drifted back to Marge.

"Gerry, do you know where he works?"

"Oh, some printing company. His dad is the shop foreman there. So he got his son a job working there with him." Gerry looked around the bar for empty glasses to be filled, and there were none, so he continued his conversation. "I hear they are very close. Danny is the only kid, and his mother died giving birth."

Marge exclaimed, "No wonder he is the way he is! You know, Gerry, those two guys are in here every day for lunch. They are regular drinking buddies. They are more like friends than father and son. I'm sure you've seen that."

"Yeah. Ed, his father, drinks an awful lot. They both do. But Ed really drinks a lot. Jesse and Art are two of the old-timers who come in often during the weekend. So I get to talk to them quite a bit. They told me they've known Ed for many years now and that it was when Ed's wife died that he took up drinking so heavy. As the years wear on, he seems to be getting worse. Some of the stories they were telling me about him were kind of funny, but they were also pretty embarrassing."

Gerry looked around and a customer caught his attention to fill a glass. He filled it and returned to Marge. "You know how gossipy those old guys get."

Marge nodded, so Gerry continued. "Well, Jesse knows somebody from where Ed works, and the report is that he has been coming to work with the smell on his breath early in the morning." Gerry paused. He seemed a little embarrassed for being so gossipy. So he added, "Fortunately, he doesn't really go overboard with the drinking until nighttime after he's done work—so far!"

This Friday evening, Marge stayed later than usual. She was enjoying her conversation with Gerry, and it was nice socializing with a few of the customers from their side of the bar. Quite a few customers walked up to her and bought her drinks in the course of their chitchat. Fortunately, for Marge, Custer's had a custom. If a customer bought another customer a drink and that customer's glass was full already, the bartender would give him or her a fancy plastic stirrer to show the next drink was paid for. That was the only time the fancy stirrers were used. They were actually display pieces with *Custer's Bar and Grill* printed in gold letters. This custom turned out to be a great idea. Customers would buy each other drinks like crazy because they didn't have to worry about the drinks getting warm or flat before the person got to drink it.

Marge had about six stirrers piled up in front of her, and for some reason, she had a premonition that the bar scene was about to get entertaining. A medium-height curly blond-headed girl came into Custer's and ordered a beer on tap. She looked like a biker, and Marge judged her to be in her early twenties. Her hair looked a bit greasy in spite of her curls, and she had on a black leather pilot's jacket.

"Well, here she is! The celebrity *scuz*!" Gerry exclaimed.

"Really? Who is she?"

"Dirty Hannah! Have you ever heard about her?"

"I've heard her name mentioned once or twice, but I never knew who she was. That's her?"

"Yep! The night's about to get interesting."

Hannah had a filthy reputation. There was quite an assortment of stories going around about her. Probably they were somewhat embellished because people like to tell stories. But one could never be sure.

Tonight Hannah set up her shop for an evening of troublemaking on the pool table side of the bar. After paying for her drink, she put her quarter down on the pool table. Then, as she coyly blew out a puff of cigarette smoke, she looked around to see who was looking. Some anonymous person whistled as if to say, "Boy, is trouble brewing tonight!"

Pool was not her real forte. Her playing was not really great. Her real game was messing with people's heads. She would shake the men up so they would miss their shots. Then if the men would get aggressive with her, she would act sexy for them. Either way, she won as far as she was concerned. She either won the game or found another fool to flirt with.

Finally her turn came up. The custom was that the winner from the previous game broke the rack. This time it was Freddie Deitz who was breaking the rack. Two balls dropped into the pockets, a high ball and a low ball. High balls are all the striped balls, and low balls are all the solid balls. The bar game was Eight Ball. The rules of playing Eight Ball were that the first player to get either a single high ball or a single low ball to drop in one of the pockets had to shoot at that group of balls for the remainder of the game, and the other player would shoot at the other group of balls. Only when a player shot all his balls into the pockets could he shoot the eight ball into a pocket. The first player to get all his or her balls and the eight ball into the pockets was the winner.

Being a shrewd player and not knowing if Hannah was sober enough to play well or not, Freddie intentionally missed his next shot just to see what she would do.

The juke box was loudly and passionately playing "Mississippi Queen." The mood was tailor-fit for her to walk up to the pool table with a cue stick in her hand and put on a show. She looked as though she was feeling just as wild as the music. She was tapping her heel on the floor so hard, she looked like she was dancing. She was obviously a little high from whatever she did previous to walking into the bar. She chalked her cue stick and eyed up the table like she really knew what she was doing. Then she dropped four balls in a row into the pockets before she finally missed. Luck just happened to be with her to make those four consecutive shots in her first try. She gave Fred a smug look. Then she nonchalantly turned around to drink her beer.

Fred was exceptionally good under pressure. If she had known, she might not have been so quick to give him the smug look. Fred calmly put his cigarette down in the ashtray. Then he eyed up the table and planned his strategy. Next he proceeded to drop his six balls and then the eight ball. Game was over. He cleared the table and won the game.

He went over to her to politely inform her, "I don't know if you knew it or not, but we're playing for beers."

She wasn't quite so polite in return. "Well, no one told me. So I'm not buying," she retorted.

Fred was not into arguing. He just shrugged his shoulders and walked away. He was just glad to get her off the table. Now the guys could get back to serious playing. As far as he was concerned, women just ruined the night when they tried to play pool.

Fred returned to his spot at the bar where his cigarette and drink were next to Danny's. Being a little curious, Dan asked him, "What was that all about?"

Fred snickered, "She won't buy me a drink. She says no one told her we were playing for drinks."

"Maybe no one did," Danny tried to reason.

Shrugging his shoulders, Fred went off to break his next rack.

Dan decided it was time to make a trip to the jukebox, right past Hannah, of course.

"Hello, sweetheart!" he said as he passed her.

Eying him up, she saw that he was heading to the juke box. She grabbed a couple of quarters from her pile of money on the bar, and followed him.

"What are you going to play?" she asked.

This, of course, led to a conversation. Next, they introduced themselves. In their conversation, Dan found out that Hannah's last name was Fowler. She was twenty-six years old. She just moved into an inexpensive apartment in Woodbury from Bellmawr, which was a couple of towns away. She used to work for the telephone company but got fired, and now she was collecting unemployment.

Marge was watching suspiciously from the other side of the bar. She just finished two of her six drinks, and now she had five more stirrers added to her pile. She obviously would not be able to drink all those drinks. But it did give her reason to stick around a little longer. Her eyes followed Hannah and Dan back to Hannah's spot at the bar.

"Hey, Gerry! When you have a minute, would you give me and the lady a drink?" Dan politely asked.

Gerry looked at Marge and rolled his eyes up.

Marge just smiled back.

Dan and Hannah were getting along nicely when Dan's turn came up on the pool table. George Bowker won the last game, and he requested to play partners so his wife Jane could play. So the next move was obvious. Dan asked Hannah to be his partner. The game turned into a long drawn-out marathon with everyone missing their shots. Jane was missing more shots than anyone.

Hearing Fred groan, Dan looked toward the bar to see him shaking his head in despair. They both laughed and turned their heads away from each other.

In the meantime, Hannah was getting very impatient. "You know, that woman is why this game is going on forever like this. Nobody is trying because she is screwing up her shots so bad." After slurping down her fifth glass of beer, Hannah was starting to get quite outspoken and loud.

George looked at Dan cocking his head in disbelief. Dan tried to stay neutral, so he just shrugged his shoulders. Jane looked upset as if she was going to cry, and then she missed another shot.

One more time, Hannah opened her mouth, "Oh, come on!"

That was it. George had it. "Shut her mouth up!"

Suddenly Dan and George were yelling at each other at the top of their lungs. George was in his late thirties and out with his wife, so he really didn't want to get into a fight. And Dan didn't usually strike anyone, unless they struck him first. He'd rather run his mouth off. So fortunately, there was not any physical violence. But Gerry couldn't allow the yelling to go on like that. He ran out from behind the bar and stood between the two men screaming at the top of his lungs, "Shut up! Both of you!"

Silence took over the whole barroom. No one would mess with Bluto Blazeuski. Everyone in the bar was at a hushed halt, waiting to see what would happen next because Gerry was known to pick up people whole and throw them out the door.

He pointed at Dan and then at George, and said, "You and you are both regular customers of this bar, and I didn't see either one of you take a swing at each other. So I'm letting you both stay. Just finish out your game without the ladies, and get it over so someone else can play."

Noticing an angry scowl on Hannah's face as he turned to go back behind the bar, he pointed at her and said, "You're a troublemaker. You start anything else, and you're flagged for good."

Hannah snapped to attention. Then after he passed her, she started to sulk and put all her change and small bills back into her pockets. She was the kind of girl who wouldn't carry a pocketbook because she thought it got in her way too much.

Dan walked up behind her and whispered in her ear, "Hey, why don't you just finish up your drink, and when we're finished with this game, I'll buy you breakfast." Hannah was instantly seduced. Chills ran up her spine as she nodded with approval.

A few minutes later, Dan dropped the eight ball and won the game. Then he went over to George, and apologized. "Listen. Man, I'm really sorry about what happened. Why don't you take over the next game? I think I'm leaving anyway."

George raised his eyebrows in a knowledgeable look and said "Okay. No hard feelings."

Then Dan and Hannah joined each other at the bar to finish up their drinks. After a few lustful gazes and some small talk, they left for the diner. On their way out, Danny's eyes locked with Marge's eyes that were staring coldly at him.

Shortly after they left, Marge left. On her way home, she passed the diner to see if Danny and Hannah were there. Sure enough! His car was in the parking lot. Then she saw them through the back windshield of the car.

"Kissing!" Marge exclaimed to herself. She couldn't believe it. She wondered if she should tell Judy about what happened tonight.

CHAPTER 5

Downward Spiral

Earlier that same Friday morning, Judy headed to the store for milk, bread, and eggs. On the bus ride into town, she gazed at the beautiful October colors. Maybe it took her mind off the harsh realities she was dealing with. As the bus neared town, she remembered she needed to pick up the prescription for her prenatal vitamins, so she stopped off at the drugstore first.

As she waited for the pharmacist to fill her prescription, she decided to have tea at the lunch counter. When she passed by the cash register at the end of the counter, she noticed a girl she knew, Cindy Boyer. Her younger sister, Loraine, went to school with Judy. At first, Judy felt a little shy. But as she passed Cindy, she said, "Hi!" However, Cindy didn't seem to hear her. So Judy said it a little louder to be sure she heard it this time: "Hi, Cindy!" But Cindy was definitely ignoring her. Realizing it was intentional, Judy felt completely humiliated. She shyly found a seat at end of the counter and ordered her usual hot tea with lemon.

As she was taking her first sip of tea, she noticed the waitress leaning over the counter to hear what Cindy was saying in a very hushed tone. "You're kidding!" she heard the waitress say. Then she saw the waitress look directly down the counter at her.

There was no doubt about it. Judy knew they were talking about her. Her cheeks blushed with shame and panic as she thought, *Oh, my goodness! I don't believe it. What am I supposed to do?* Even though she didn't look pregnant yet, apparently the rumor was out, and Cindy was busy telling everyone about it at the pharmacy counter. Judy stared out the window, pretending not to pay any attention to them. Finally they stopped whispering and started speaking in normal voices. Now she could hear every word they were saying.

Cindy began to talk about how good she was doing at her job as teller at the bank. "They're so happy with me; they put me in charge of the drive-up window."

Listen to her brag, Judy thought to herself.

"Oh, yeah?" she heard the waitress reply.

"Yeah, well, I guess I'm where I'm supposed to be because I always was good with numbers. I got the math award when I graduated from high school last year."

"Hm-m," was the waitress's rather cool reply as they continued with their small talk.

In the meantime, Judy was still in agony from her humiliation. *How do I walk past those two to pay for my tea?* With her cheeks still burning, Judy fumbled through her purse to find the change to pay for her tea. She made sure not to leave a tip. *Snotty thing doesn't deserve it,* she said to herself.

As she made her way past Cindy to the register, she heard her snorting in laughter. Her hand trembled lightly as the waitress approached. She placed her money and check on the counter to be rung up in the register. She could feel the waitress taking her complete personal and moral inventory as she put the money into the register. Judy looked away the whole time. Then she headed to the other side of the pharmacy to the retail counter to pick up and pay for her prenatal vitamins. She never looked back as she was leaving. And as she walked out the door the tears, that she had been fighting back, began to trickle down her cheeks.

Judy quickly finished her errands in town and headed home. All the way home on the bus, she struggled to keep her composure. She was wracked with anger and hatred for Cindy and the waitress, humiliated over her condition, and full of fear about what kind of rumors could be circulating around town about her being pregnant. She was sure she would never be able to show her face in town again.

When she arrived home, she numbly put away the groceries. Then she broke into big sobs. It just seemed to her like the whole world was against her. After crying for a while, she decided to put on the television. Maybe this would get her mind off all these terrible burdens. Then a commercial came on that threw her back into a crying jag. It was a very emotional plea to the general public showing orphaned children. It expressed that many of the children were illegitimate and unwanted. It then showed the lonely faces of rejected children and asked the general public to make donations or adopt.

Immediately Judy's thoughts turned to the illegitimate child developing in her own womb. Her crying process swelled and ebbed again as she rubbed her belly and spoke to the baby. "I'm so sorry, baby. I wish I did things the right way. Maybe there's still hope. Maybe your dumb father will still marry me and make things all right for you."

The crying went on all afternoon until late that evening when Marge came home from her interesting evening at the bar. As Marge approached the house, she was still contemplating whether or not she should tell Judy about Danny leaving the bar with Hannah. As she opened the front door, there was Judy with her box of tissues in hand.

"Hi! What's up?" Marge asked, hoping Judy was just crying over a sad show on the television.

"I don't want to talk about it."

"Well, I can see you're upset about something. And if you're this upset, I think you should talk about it," Marge replied as she went to the bedroom to hang up her sweater.

Returning to Judy on the sofa, Marge sat down. Downcast, Judy then told Marge the story of her whole day, including the television commercial.

Putting her arms around Judy, Marge tried her best to console her. "Look! I don't think all this crying is very good for the baby. And you can't let people bother you like that."

Judy continued crying.

"Would you like a cup of tea or some instant coffee? I had a few drinks after work tonight, and maybe a cup of coffee would do me good."

Judy pursed her lips and nodded to indicate she wanted some.

As Marge started the water boiling, she tried to encourage Judy by telling her, "You know, those girls really are not worth crying over. By the way, do you want tea or coffee?"

"You know I always drink tea, Marge. I know, but it seems everywhere I go, I get looks. And I know how Cindy is. She'll be sure to tell everyone she knows. I feel so paranoid. Now I know how a retarded kid must feel when people make fun of him."

"Really now, Judy, stop thinking those kinds of thoughts and try to calm down."

"You know what really eats at me? It's not just me that will suffer for my stupidity, but my baby will too! We'll both be social outcasts!" With that, Judy broke out into heavy sobbing again. "Oh, I wish I listened to Mom and waited until I got married. If only Danny would care enough for the baby to marry me, things would be different."

Marge's back was turned to Judy as she said this. Her eyebrows both shot up. Her first impulse was to tell Judy the story about what she saw in the bar tonight. Her thoughts weighed heavily on her as she took the coffee cups down from the cupboard. She muttered to herself, "I've got to tell her. She's got to give up on that creep."

She brought the tea and coffee over and set them down on the coffee table. As she sat erectly on the sofa next to Judy, Marge carefully collected her words and composure. "Judy, why don't you give up on Danny?"

Judy shot an angry look at her. "Maybe he'll change!"

Marge let out a deep breath and tried again. "Do you honestly think he will still pull through like a fairytale and marry you and make a home for you and the baby?"

"Yeah! Why not?" Judy shot back indignantly. "The baby is his responsibility too!"

Marge let Judy have both barrels of the gun. "You know, I saw him leave the bar tonight with some skanky girl named Hannah. What kind of interest do you think he could have in you and the baby if he's doing stuff like that? And would you really want to be married to someone who sleeps around on you like that?"

"What?" Judy jumped up from the sofa.

Marge pulled her back down on the sofa. "Yeah! Then I saw him and her at the diner afterward."

Judy tried to jump up again, but Marge pulled her down. "Kissing!"

Judy jumped up for the final time, shrieking sobs. She managed to break away from Marge's grip this time and ran for her little bedroom. Marge headed toward the bedroom after her, but paused. She began to feel bad for telling Judy about Danny, but then she decided it was better for Judy to know now instead of continuing on in foolish hopes. So Marge left Judy alone to cry it all out of her system and hopefully pull herself together later.

All through the night, Judy continued to sob bitterly. Thrown across her bed with her box of tissues, her first thought was how could she get out of this terrible situation? As her thoughts milled around in her head, she came to the conclusion that outside of aborting the baby, there was no easy way out.

She faced the fact that Danny was not very likely to be her knight in shining armor. She wished she could just die or run away to get out of this mess. *How can this be?* she thought as her crying slowed down. *Marge wouldn't make up a story like that. Especially when she knew I felt so bad already. She's just trying to make me see the truth. She's probably right. It's useless to hope that Danny will change. I should have listened to Mom.*

Immobilizing depression began to set in. *Gee! Mom's done with me. So she doesn't care. Danny doesn't care. No one cares. If I didn't know better, I'd think that Marge doesn't even care.* Finally, Judy fell asleep right where she lay, flopped across the bed, until the following morning.

Marge had trouble sleeping herself. As she lay in her bed, her mind whirled with a hundred thoughts. *Judy doesn't seem to realize it, but she will survive. So will the baby. We all make mistakes, and somehow things still seem to work out. Who needs that scumbag anyway?* Marge reassured herself that Judy had to know what kind of person Danny was so she could get on with reality. Somehow her mind drifted to her conversation with the principal a couple of weeks previously. She thought out loud, "I wonder if we could get her into counseling. Maybe it would help her." Marge made a mental note to be sure to discuss this with Judy tomorrow.

The following morning, Judy dragged herself to the kitchen table and dropped into her chair.

"Judy, Mr. Dumont suggested you might be interested in going to a counselor or having a tutor come so you could work on your GED."

"Forget it! I'm not going out unless I have to, and I don't want to see anyone. Anyone! I hate myself, and I just wish I could die!" Judy was in a state of dismal depression.

Marge sighed. Then she suggested, "Maybe a counselor could help you feel better. You've got to stop beating yourself up. Maybe you could still finish school. You don't have to be a loser just because you feel like one today." After a short pause, Marge went on, "You know feelings are not facts. Just because you feel like everyone is looking down at you doesn't mean they are."

It didn't help. Judy just spent the rest of the day speechless and distant.

CHAPTER 6

Making Some Progress

Almost all the flamboyant colors of fall were gone. It was early November. Everything seemed brown and ended. Judy was surviving with her situation, but she was feeling very down.

The mailman pulled away from the mailbox, and Judy looked out the window just in time to see him disappear around the withered cornfield. "I hope that welfare check has arrived," she said as she put on her heavy sweater to go out to get the mail. She was a little over three months pregnant now. Even though she didn't quite look pregnant, she noticed that her jeans were a little tighter, and she looked better if she didn't button her sweater all the way down.

She looked up to heaven, blurting a quick prayer as she was opening the mailbox. She took a deep breath as she looked in. It was there. The envelope from the welfare office was there! Clutching the rest of the mail, she ran into the house. She didn't even take her sweater off. She put all the mail but the piece from the welfare office down on the table and opened it.

"No check?" Judy's heart sank. There was a letter inside telling her she was eligible, but she needed a legally responsible relative to receive her checks for her. "Oh no! Now what do I do? Mom won't want to help," Judy almost choked, remembering her disbelief the day when she threatened to run away, and her mother told her to just go. Judy very much regretted her bad behavior that day. With nowhere else to go, she walked five miles to Marge's house, not even knowing if Marge was home. That event with her mother was a very upsetting eye-opener for Judy. She so regretted getting herself pregnant, and she so regretted the way she behaved with her mother that day. Her heart broke to think what a mess she made of her life and that of her baby just because she made such bad choices with her young life.

Judy wanted to cry, but she knew that wouldn't help. She decided she was going to act grownup this time. She took her sweater off and started boiling water for tea. She muttered to herself, "I'll call Marge at work. But she probably wouldn't know what to do either. Besides, I don't want her to see me as a wimpy baby who can't be responsible."

She opened the cupboard to get down a teacup. "There's got to be something I can do—some other way." Then a thought struck her. *Ronnie! That nice lady at the welfare office. If anyone would know, she would.* She put the cup back in the cupboard, turned off the tea water, grabbed her heavy sweater and purse, and charged out the door.

After getting off the bus, she ran excitedly up the stairs, anxiously looking to see if Ronnie was sitting at her desk. "Ronnie!" she hollered.

Startled Ronnie jumped in her chair when she heard her name. Then she saw Judy running up the stairs. "Yes, dear!"

"Oh, Ronnie! I've got to talk to you."

"Certainly! Have a seat!" she motioned Judy to sit down next to her desk.

"I've got to ask you something. I just got a letter in the mail today saying I'm eligible for welfare, but I needed a legally responsible relative to receive my check for me."

"Isn't that something? You're old enough to have a baby but you're not old enough to collect a check from the state. Oh my!" Ronnie chuckled ruefully. Then she asked, "So why can't one of your parents get it for you?"

"Oh no! My mom told me to leave, and I don't think she wants anything to do with me." She paused then said, "And my dad's dead."

"What about your sister? Didn't you say before that you were living with your sister?"

"Marge? But doesn't she have to be my legal guardian?"

"How old is she?"

"Twenty-three."

"That's old enough!" Ronnie said with a reassuring smile. "New Jersey law says you just need to have either a parent, legal guardian, or an adult relative who is living with you that is at least eighteen years old to be the payee on your behalf."

"Wow! I don't believe it's that simple. Are you sure?" Judy queried.

Ronnie was chuckling now. "Absolutely! But you'll have to go to the services department and discuss it with them first. They will tell you exactly what you and your sister need to do."

"Okay. Where are they?"

"Down the hall. You'll see their sign."

Judy jumped up from her seat and grabbed Ronnie to hug her as hard as she could. Surprised, Ronnie laughed as she hugged her back. "Well, you better go take care of business."

"Okay." Judy picked up her purse and headed down the hall. The representative in the services department told Judy to simply have Marge come in with her and fill out the papers.

Judy had to pass Ronnie on her way out. So she stopped in the doorway to say, "Good-bye." Then she threw Ronnie a kiss and said "Thanks again!"

"Oh! I'm just glad I could be here to help you. Maybe you can come in to see me once you have your baby. I would love to see the baby and to see how you both are doing."

"You got it! Thanks again for your help! Bye!"

"Bye, dear!" Ronnie smiled as Judy bounced down the steps.

Judy arrived home shortly before Marge and was feeling quite pleased with herself for being able to find a good solution to her problem. "Gee! That wasn't so bad. I handled that pretty good. Maybe things can work out after all."

Marge's car pulled up in front of the house. When Marge came in, Judy told her everything that happened.

"Okay. I'll talk to Buddy tomorrow about letting me go for a couple of hours to square it away." Pausing, Marge turned her head to look at Judy, "Gee! You did good, kid!" Then she smiled to herself knowing that Judy was probably benefiting from that emotional pat.

Early on the following morning, Marge got permission from Buddy to run a few blocks down the street and take care of business at the welfare office. On her way out, she stopped in the phone booth just outside of the bar and called her mother.

"Hi, Mom!"

"Hi, Marge! How's everything going?"

"As good as can be expected."

"Is something the matter?" her mother asked in a worried tone.

"No, Mom! Nothing to be worried about. Judy is having a bit of a hard time with herself. Up until a few weeks ago, she still had hopes that Danny would marry her. And you know he won't. He's just a creep!

"Oh, well. She will learn eventually." Her mother paused and went on, "By the way, everything at school is taken care of. She is officially signed out. Also, the principal, Mr. Dumont, asked if we would be interested in any tutoring or counseling for Judy. I told him I didn't think so. But maybe it is something that you should mention to her."

"No way, Mom! I already asked her." Marge's voice droned on, "She doesn't want to see anyone. She rarely even leaves the house. She is so afraid of what people are going to say about her. Do you remember that snotty Cindy Boyer?"

"Oh yes! Loraine's older sister."

"Yes. Judy went to the drugstore one afternoon and somehow Cindy must have caught hold of the rumor that Judy was pregnant and made a point of putting her down and embarrassing her in front of other people." Then Marge rambled on to the next unhappy scenario, "Then, when she was still pining about Danny, I told her about how I saw Danny leave the bar with some really scuzzy girl …"

Her mother cut in, "Oh! How could you?"

"Mom, I had to! She kept hanging her dreams on this creep, and he couldn't care less about her. She really needed to get in touch with reality."

"I guess you're right," her mother commented doubtfully.

"I'm on my way to the welfare office. Judy applied, and they told her she could only collect if she has a legally responsible relative living with her to receive the check on her behalf. They also told her that I'm eligible to be that relative. I was surprised because I thought I would have to be her legal guardian. But not so. I only need to be a relative over eighteen who she happens to be living with and can act as her payee. Interesting, huh?"

"Well, yes it is. Very interesting! In the meantime, do you need any money or food?"

"Yeah! We can use the money more than the food. She actually qualified for food stamps, which have been helping out a lot. And thankfully, she had no problem qualifying for Medicaid either. But since she's been here a while now with no money coming in, money has been a little tight." Marge's thoughts drifted to how giving her mother really was and how she jumped right in with an offer to help without even being asked. Then she suddenly remembered Judy complaining that the *big* clothes given her before were getting a little tight. So she asked, "Mom, if you can find some regular maternity blouses and pants, she could use that, too. Those nice, loose clothes you gave her before are starting to get tight."

"I'll head down to the thrift shop at the church this morning to see what maternity clothes I can find. Then I'll bring them over a little later, along with some money. Where will you be this afternoon?"

Marge chewed her lip. "I'll be back at Custer's." Even though she very much appreciated her mother's help, she still had to restrain her pride at the thought of accepting the financial help from her mother. Marge still wanted to be the self-sufficient hero, but she knew she had no choice. She needed the help.

"Okay. I'll leave it all in your car like I did the last time. The money will be in your glove box, okay? I'm not coming in. You know how I feel about places like that, Marge."

Marge's brow knitted. She knew in her heart that her mother certainly did not approve of her working in a bar, especially if she wasn't willing to set foot in such a place. "Okay, Mom. Thanks a lot."

"Later on, I'll get out the sewing machine and make some maternity clothes to drop off."

"Wow! That's great, Mom. Thanks!" Then Marge remembered how her mother would always pray, and it always seemed that God gave her whatever she asked for. So after a brief pause, Marge added, "Oh, and Mom, please pray for her. Judy's been so down in spirit. She worries me from seeing her so depressed all the time."

"Don't worry, dear. I have been." Her mother's voice seemed to carry a note of pleasure at the request for prayer. After all those years of Marge putting on such a strong front and not really wanting anything to do with God, her heart seemed to be softening. So her mother took a chance on reaching out to her daughter to try to rebuild the relationship. "Marge, maybe we can get together sometime?"

"Okay, Mom! Maybe one day after work we can go to the Chinese place nearby." Marge was surprised by her mother's suggestion. She was even more surprised by the longing she felt to spend time with her mother.

After Marge and her mother were done talking, she headed directly to the welfare office. Marge and Judy had prearranged that Judy would take the bus and meet Marge there. So Judy was already there waiting anxiously as she sat and talked to her friend, Ronnie.

They finished up business quickly and were assured that Judy's check would be coming soon. Then Marge headed back to work.

CHAPTER 7

Reality Checks

At the print shop where Dan Schisler worked, everyone was feeling very lighthearted. It was the Wednesday before Thanksgiving, and for the afternoon coffee break his father, Ed Schisler, who was the shop foreman, decided everyone should have an office party for the last hour and a half to begin celebrating the holiday early. The print shop management, who owned several print shops in the area, wasn't known to be especially generous to the employees with benefits and holidays. However, Thanksgiving was a holiday when the employees got a four-day weekend, and Ed took the liberty of starting his celebrating early.

He popped open one of three bottles of wine that he had been keeping in one of the file cabinet drawers and poured out eight clear, plastic cups full of wine for himself, Dan, and the other six employees. "To the management and to Thanksgiving!" Ed raised his cup up to make a toast, and all the other employees did the same.

Danny, however, was feeling rather uncertain. He worried about whether his father would make a fool out of himself today. Lately his father's drinking had been carried to excess on a regular basis. Fortunately, it was late in the day, so if he did go on one of his escapades, it should not get bad until the evening. So most likely he wouldn't be embarrassing Danny at work. Interestingly enough, no one at work seemed to pay much attention to Ed's drinking problem. Maybe it just wasn't so important to them. Or maybe it was because he was their boss. Whatever their reasoning was didn't matter to Danny. He was more concerned that his father's drinking could be getting to be a serious problem, and he especially didn't want it to become a problem in the workplace. Looking ahead to the Thanksgiving weekend was also a concern for Dan because for the entire Thanksgiving weekend, his father would probably be drunk right through to late Sunday night. And the only reason he would stop then was because it was time to get some sleep so he could be fit enough to return to work Monday morning. Sadly enough, it wasn't just the Thanksgiving weekend that went like that. Ed drank away almost every holiday the same way. Holidays were not only worrisome for Danny, but they were also lonely times.

Dan was well aware why his father was like this every holiday. He knew his father suffered great depression because of grieving over his dead wife, Beth. He would always tell Danny how he wished she was there to enjoy these times with them. Maybe Ed had an especially difficult time letting go of his sorrow because he grew up as an orphan. To make life even more lonely, the only relatives Dan and his father had were Beth's family, and they lived far away in England, which is where Ed and Beth met while he was in the service. As a result, Ed and Dan were pretty much alone in the world. They just had each other. And Ed's depression made holidays hard for both the father and the son.

Danny also had other reasons for feeling quite uncomfortable. He wasn't quite sure why, but he wanted like crazy to scratch his private spots. He tried to ignore it, thinking it wasn't anything to be overly concerned about. He thought the wine would help get rid of the discomfort, but it didn't.

Later that night, Danny had trouble sleeping. The itching had now turned to burning and swelling, and he kept waking up because of it. After getting up several times, he tried to rouse his father, but he was crashed out on the couch and wouldn't budge. As the morning started to break, Danny's discomfort got more and more unbearable.

Friday morning, he couldn't wait for the doctor to get into his office. Every fifteen minutes he called the office from 6:30 a.m. on, until he finally got the answering service around 8:00 a.m.

"Doctor Anderson's answering service," was the reply on the phone.

"When will the doctor be in?" Danny impatiently queried.

"Oh, he's off today, but he'll come in if it's an emergency."

Danny almost wanted to cry. "Believe me. It's an emergency!"

"What's your name?"

"Dan Schisler."

"What is your problem?"

"If you don't mind, I'd rather tell the doctor." Dan was too embarrassed to tell her.

"Oh, okay!" the voice replied sarcastically. "I'll call him at home, and you should be hearing from him sometime this morning."

"Please, make it quick. Tell him I can't wait.," Danny begged.

At 9:00 a.m. Danny still didn't hear from the doctor. So he called the answering service again. Finally, just before 9:30 a.m., the phone rang.

"Hello. This is Doctor Anderson. Is Dan Schisler there?"

"Oh, doctor, it is so good to hear from you." He paused in embarrassment for a couple of seconds, then went on, "Uh, my privates have been burning and swelling since yesterday, and it just seems to keep getting worse. I'm really distressed about this. I can't wait until the next day your office is open. Can you please see me today?"

"Well," the doctor answered rather coolly, "I guess the sooner the better. How soon can you get into the office?"

"I'll come in right now if you want. Like you said, the sooner the better. Do you have any idea what the problem is?"

"Well, that's hard to say until I see you. It could be any number of things. It could be a urinary tract infection. It could be from a girl you've been seeing. Or it could be something else, and I really can't tell you until I see you in my office."

"Oh!" Danny replied, sounding quite stunned.

"Well, uh-hum-m-m," the doctor thoughtfully cleared his throat. "If you come in right away, I'll see you in about twenty minutes at my office."

Dan told him he'd be there waiting for him, and he darted out the door. On his way to the doctor's office, Danny thought to himself, *I bet I got something from that lowlife, Hannah!* His fierce lust of the last few weeks quickly dwindled into shame and remorse. "Man! How could I let this happen to me? When my friends find out, they'll all be laughing at me." He pictured his friend, Fred, who liked to joke around with him. "Well, now he'll really have something to rib me about!" He started to chuckle as he thought about Fred teasing him over this. Then he considered more deeply. "If only I restrained myself and did the right thing, I wouldn't be in this fix." His thoughts continued on to Judy. "If I behaved myself with Judy, she wouldn't be pregnant, and I wouldn't be having an illegitimate child. Man, I've been messing up right and left. I've got to stop fooling around like this. I'm not doing good at all."

As Danny entered the doctor's office, his thoughts were back on his father, who was drunk and had no idea of what was going on. Anger boiled up as he mumbled to himself, "Where are you at a time like this when it would really be nice to have someone to talk to about this? But you're just too drunk to even know what's going on."

"Danny, come on in." Dr. Anderson led Danny right past the receptionist's desk because no one was there but the two of them since the office was officially closed for the holiday. Danny was rather relieved about the convenience of the timing of his event. He didn't really want to feel like he had to explain himself to anyone over his ailment.

After examining Danny, the doctor asked if Danny had any intercourse recently. Danny sheepishly confirmed that he did. The doctor concluded that the problem was gonorrhea and gave Danny a shot of penicillin and a prescription for more penicillin to follow.

"You would do well to let that girl know that she's infected," the doctor told him.

"Thanks. I will, Doc." Danny said with a red face as he went on. "Thanks for coming in on your day off just for me. I'd be in real trouble if you weren't available."

"Oh, you're quite welcome," said the doctor as he repressed a smile.

Once Danny got into his car, he rubbed his face trying to cool down the burning blush. "Oh man! How embarrassing!" he muttered to himself as he made a beeline to the nearest drugstore. On his way there, he made a firm commitment to have nothing to do with Hannah ever again. He decided he wasn't going to tell her she gave him an infection either. He figured she must already know she has it. "Imagine how many other people got it because of her," he thought out loud. "What a disgusting pig!" Danny also made a firm commitment to himself that he would be much more discriminating about the girls he got involved with from there on.

When he got to the drugstore, the woman who took care of the retail counter took his prescription to give to the pharmacist. Dan grew leery. He knew her. It was the mother of some girl from work, Mrs. Webber.

"Are you sick, Danny?" she asked.

"Oh, it's nothing serious. I just got a little bug," he said as he held his stomach as if in pain.

From there, he went over to the luncheon counter to have a cup of coffee and wait for his prescription to be filled. Fortunately he didn't know the waitress at the counter and could sit in peace to drink his coffee.

He rubbed his eyes with the palms of his hands as he thought to himself, *This is incredible. Imagine that! She gave me a venereal disease.* He wanted to rub his privates to ease the discomfort but instead he just shifted in his seat. His thoughts rambled on. *She wasn't even worth all this bother. I never really thought very much of her, and I doubt if she ever really cared very much about me either. She was definitely not worth all this distress.* Dan felt rather upset with himself for making such poor choices.

His thoughts briefly turned to Judy. *What a sweet girl she is. She's the kind of girl that I should have been going after. Not someone like Hannah.* He felt a lump in his throat as he remembered how he left her standing there bawling her eyes out when she told him she was pregnant. His conscience disturbed him, and he thought about how she felt when he walked away from her. Then he started to think about the baby. His own father often bemoaned the fact that he was orphaned and never got to know his parents. *At least*, he thought, *my baby will know his mother because I doubt if she would ever put him up for adoption.* Guilt started to take over. Thoughts about abandoning his baby much like his father's parents abandoned him struck his heart with deep remorse. He tried to shake all the negative thoughts out of his head, but he couldn't. He just plain felt depressed at this point. He tapped his spoon on the counter with one loud tap as he quietly mumbled to himself, "But I'm just not ready for getting married and having children yet."

The waitress came over and looked into his annoyed face. "Did you want something?"

"No." Dan realized his feelings were showing and laughed with mild bravado, "I was just thinking. Sorry!"

His thoughts continued to plague him as the waitress walked away. *I left that sweet girl crying like that. And in the meantime, I may have just left her life and my child's life in ruins.* That was it. He had to leave so he could get away from all these miserable thoughts. He paid for his coffee and went back to the retail counter to see if his prescription was ready. He was quite grateful to find that it was.

CHAPTER 8

The Robbery

Early in December, Judy made her usual anxious trek to the mailbox, hoping that she would find a check. This was almost the only time she would go out of the house. She was so afraid of meeting someone who would know her that she stayed in the house as much as possible. She wouldn't even go to the store. Marge had to do the grocery shopping on her way home from work.

Mumbling her ritual prayer, "Oh, God, please let it be in there," she opened the mailbox. An envelope from welfare was in there. She didn't even wait to go back into the house to open it. As she opened the envelope she saw the edge of the check. "Yeah! It's here! Oh, thank you, God! Thank you, God!" She grabbed up the rest of the mail and ran into the house.

She was so relieved and happy, she couldn't even wait for Marge to come home. She called her up at work to tell her. "Marge, there isn't just one check, but two. One for this month and one for last month!"

That night, they both rejoiced. Marge brought home a pizza and soda to celebrate.

A couple of weeks later, it was getting closer to Christmas time. Judy's spirits picked up even more since money wasn't so tight now, and there were reminders of the holidays all around. Judy actually felt good enough to forget about her shame and embarrassment for a little bit and go into town to Christmas shop. She only got a few simple gifts: a sweater for Marge, perfume for Mom, and a teddy bear for the baby. Then she had an afterthought and went back into the store to get some cheap aftershave for her mother's boyfriend.

When she returned to the cottage, her heart was warmed by the sight. Their home was quaintly decorated with a skinny, fake tree decorated and lighted in the front window so you could see it from the road. And there was a plastic Santa Claus face on the front door. As she went inside, there was a Christmas centerpiece on the kitchen table and some Christmas cards that Marge brought home from work that were strung so they hung nicely across the tops of the curtains.

As Judy was wrapping gifts in the kitchen, she had a long-playing record joyously trumpeting Christmas music on the record player in the living room. Her spirits hadn't been this good in months. She finished wrapping Marge's gift first, so she could hide it away before Marge came home. When she started to wrap her mother's gift, her spirits took a momentary dip. "I wonder if I'll get to see her for Christmas." Resigned not to get depressed after feeling so good all day, she told herself, *At least I am prepared if I do see her. And if I don't, I will mail it to her, and she will know that I was thinking about her.*

She was doing a good job of stuffing her feelings. However, the reality was that she was still deeply wounded by the fact that her mother told her to leave. Judy justified her mother's actions by telling herself that she deserved it. But there was still an empty ache in her heart, wondering if her mother still loved her or would ever forgive her for being such a miserable, ornery kid and for getting pregnant the way she did.

She chuckled to herself as she wrapped the aftershave for her mother's boyfriend. "I bet they'll both be surprised. I hope they like their gifts."

In the meantime, while Judy was at home preparing and shopping for Christmas, Marge was at work noticing something very peculiar. A strange man kept walking past the door of the bar and looking in. He walked by and did this several times. She didn't know who he was and was feeling very suspicious.

Pops Wagner, who was one of the regular old-timers, mentioned that he heard that more robberies happen just before the holidays. He said, "I heard on the news yesterday that during the holidays, people get desperate. They want to give their poor families a nice holiday but don't have the money. So they resort to stealing it."

Pops was eighty-two years old. So Marge usually just humored him because he was an old man. But this time, his comments made her very nervous.

When it got close to lunch, the man disappeared for a while. Jesse, another old-timer, reassured her, "Don't worry. He's gone now. I've been keeping my eyes on the front of the place, and I haven't seen him for a while now."

The bar started to fill up for lunch. Buddy came out to help her with the busy crowd. With the Christmas holidays being just barely a couple of weeks away, the bar seemed to get much busier. Not only were there more customers, but they bought each other a lot more drinks to celebrate the soon approaching Christmas holiday. The crowd also lingered a little longer than usual. Finally around 3:00 p.m., the bar slowed down. Buddy emptied all the big bills and checks out from under the money tray in the cash register. "Wow! With today's lunch rush, we made a killing," he said as he headed to the kitchen to count it and prepare the deposit to take to the bank. Once he was done putting his deposit together, he headed out to the bank.

Buddy wasn't even gone five minutes when someone ran into the bar with a ski mask on and a gun in his hand. He made a beeline behind the bar, grabbed Marge by the arm, and put the gun to her head. "Don't no one move, or I'll blow her brains out."

There were only perhaps a dozen customers in the bar—five of the old-timers, Pops, Jesse, Jack, Art, and Arnie; plus about six or seven younger guys at the pool table. Marge's eyes scanned to see who the younger guys were at the pool table to identify if any of them were troublemakers. At least three of the young guys happened to be roughnecks in the bar at one time or another. All she could think about was that one of them might decide to become gallant and foolish at her expense. Inwardly, Marge was praying, "Oh God, please help me! Oh God, please help me!"

She could feel the robber's hand, which was holding her arm tightly, shake as he commanded her to open the cash register. He then told her to put the money into a paper bag. She reached under the cash register for a paper bag. Trembling, she put the money into the bag.

"All of it!" he shouted at her.

"Take it easy on her," one of the young guys shouted at the robber.

Marge gulped as the robber told him, "Shut up if you don't want me to shoot her brains out on you." After that, the whole bar was deadly silent.

"Take the tray out," he told her, "and give me the money from under the tray too."

Marge took out the tray. There were only four twenties.

"Is that all there is?" he bellowed at her.

Marge started crying, "Please don't hurt me. Buddy just cleaned out the drawer after lunch and took the money to the bank."

"So that's why he left," the robber thought out loud. Apparently the robber might have thought Buddy's leaving was his opportunity to do his dirty work.

Marge tried to look at the guy to see if there was anything she could identify about him. He had on a ski mask. His eyes were brown. He was medium height, about five foot, eight or nine inches. That's all she could tell. She was too scared to remember anything else. She handed him the bag; he grabbed it and backed away from her and then charged out the door and was gone.

As Marge was stumbling toward the phone in the kitchen, Pops hollered out, "Call the police. Right away!"

"Yeah!" Marge said as her fingers numbly dialed the police.

Five minutes later, the police and Buddy pulled up to the bar at the same time.

"What's the matter?" Buddy asked.

He knew this wasn't just another barroom brawl. The officers both had very serious looks on their faces, looks that were not the scowling or sneering annoyance they give when they're there for a barroom fight.

They all ran into the bar to find all the old-timers huddled around Marge as she was throwing a shot of brandy down her throat.

"What's going on?" Buddy shouted out in distress.

"Oh, Buddy, while you were gone, we were robbed!" Marge cried out.

"Holy cow! Are you all right?" Buddy's face turned pale with shock.

"Yeah! Outside of being shaken to death! The guy held a gun to my head and threatened to blow my brains out."

One of the police officers cut in, "Did he hurt you physically?"

"No. He grabbed my arm pretty hard. But I'm all right."

"Do you remember what he looked like?"

Marge gave the police officers the description the best that she could. But she couldn't remember the color of his clothes. It all happened so fast that some of it was a blur. She was still shaking. After she answered all the police's questions that she could, she told Buddy she had to go home. There was only a half an hour to her shift left anyway, so Buddy didn't mind. He could very easily see that Marge was quite badly shaken up by this event.

"Will you be all right driving home, sweetheart?" Buddy asked with kindest concern.

"I think so," Marge stuttered. "I'll have Judy call you when I get home."

"Good girl!" Buddy replied. As she headed out, Buddy went over to listen in on the police for further details as they interviewed all the customers in the bar who were present during the robbery. Buddy had a lot of crazy things happen in his bar but never before was there a robbery.

CHAPTER 9

Healing Begins

When Marge arrived home, Judy was just putting away the wrapping paper. "Marge! You're home early!" she remarked. Then she stopped short. She could see by the look on Marge's face that something was wrong. "What's the matter?"

"I'll tell you in a minute. First call Buddy at work and tell him I got home okay."

Judy did what she was told with her mouth hung open with shock. As soon as she hung up the phone, she said, "So what happened? You look like you had a close call with death."

"That's not funny! I did have a close call with death!" Marge snapped back.

"What?" Judy was flabbergasted. A few minutes ago she was happily wrapping Christmas presents. Now Marge was telling her she had a close call with death.

"Some jerk came into the bar with a gun, held it to my head, and robbed us." Marge then proceeded to give Judy all the details.

"Did they catch the guy?"

"I don't know. Who cares? I'm so disgusted; I don't care about anything anymore."

Now Judy was really stunned. She was puzzled over what she should do next. Here was an opportunity for her to be consoling to Marge instead of vice versa, and she didn't know what to say. Numbly, she just put her arms around Marge and didn't say much except, "I'm glad you're all right."

"Judy, would you make me some coffee? I'm going to take a shower, put on my night robe, and just sit quiet tonight."

"No dinner?" Judy wondered.

"No. I really don't feel like eating. I just need to calm down."

"Well, if you need to calm down, how about tea instead? It would probably be more calming than a cup of coffee with all that caffeine in it."

Marge consented. So Judy started the tea water. While the tea water was heating up, she tried to think what she could do to make Marge feel better, and she remembered she had some homemade Christmas cookies hidden away in a tin can. She amused herself because she remembered her mother doing that exact same kind of thing, and now she was doing just what her mother would do.

Well, it's really not a good dinner, but at least, it's food, Judy thought as she set the cookies and Marge's tea down on the coffee table. Then she tried to find a good show on the television for Marge, but there was nothing good on but the news and a Christmas show with singing and dancing. *At least it's happy,* she thought. *Maybe it'll help,* as she tried to tune in the channel to see the Christmas show a little better.

Marge came out and Judy directed her to where she should sit as if she were directing a queen to a throne. Then she encouraged Marge to put her feet up on the coffee table next to the cookies.

As she was settling into her seat, Marge softly said, "Judy, thanks so much for being so nice to me. I'm so glad you're here tonight. It's really helps to know that someone who cares is here right now. You have no idea how much it means to me to have my sweet little sister here to comfort me at a time like this."

Judy was so pleased to hear this from Marge. It made her feel good to be of such comfort. As she went to sit on the other end of the sofa, she looked into Marge's eyes to say, "You're welcome," but instead, she said, "Marge, were you crying or something? Your eyes are red." She wasn't used to seeing Marge cry because she was always such a strong person whom no one would expect to ever cry.

Marge sighed, "Yeah. You know sometimes I really feel like I can't take it anymore. This job is hard enough putting up with all the drunks and their problems, but what happened today is like the straw that broke the camel's back. I'm starting to hate this job."

"Marge, I had no idea you didn't like your job."

"After a while, it gets to you. And I guess it's been building up on me." She paused and then said, "I didn't really want to weigh you down with all this because you've been struggling with your own problems so much already."

"Well, maybe it's time to find another job," Judy thoughtfully replied.

"I don't know what else I can do and make the money I'm making right now. We have to eat and pay bills and rent. So for now, I'm kind of stuck until I find something better."

"Oh Marge! There's got to be something you can do besides working at Custer's."

"I guess," Marge halfheartedly replied. "I will be looking around. But in the meantime, I will keep working at Custer's until I do find something better." Marge continued on, "You know, since I've taken this job at Custer's, I think I understand a little better what makes Mom tick."

"Yeah?" Judy seemed intrigued by what Marge would reveal next.

"Yeah. I couldn't understand why she didn't take a firmer stand with Dad with all his drinking. After working at Custer's, I think I know. You just can't reason with a drunk. And if someone wants to drink himself to death, there's nothing you can do about it. You can't stop or control him. If you try, you just drive yourself crazy. It doesn't make sense. I mean, why would anyone want to destroy himself? But some people just do, and no one can stop them."

Judy rubbed her earlobe as she remembered out loud, "I recall asking Dad why he drank so much, and he said he liked it because he liked the way it made him feel. You know, Marge, I really think Dad had that heart attack because he drank so much. I remember how sometimes his face would get so red just from having one beer, without even doing anything. That was not a good sign."

"Yeah, I know," Marge sighed. "You know, Mom really had to be a very strong person to have been able to live with him all those years. I always used to think she didn't have a spine when he used to come home and curse at her, or worse still, come home late at night and wake up the whole house with his stumbling and bellowing. She would never say a thing, except maybe once in a while, she would sigh. I used to think she should holler and give him a good rebuking or something to make him shape up his act. But you know what? Anyone can holler and make a scene. But why bother if it's not going to change anything or worse yet it just makes situations worse? As I said, Mom must be a really strong person because it takes a strong person to stand so strong and maintain her sanity while living with all that."

"Oh yeah?" Judy quipped. "You should have seen how strong Mom was the day she stood up to me and told me to leave. I never thought she would do it, especially after how she put up with Dad all those years."

"Okay, Judy. Stop right there. For Dad, who was a hopeless alcoholic, there was nothing that could move him to change. But you're a young girl, and maybe Mom thought that if you had to pay the consequences for your behavior, you would learn something." Judy was silent. Marge could see by her long face that Judy didn't believe it. "What? You think Mom doesn't care anymore?"

"I don't know, Marge. Either that or she didn't want to put up with the aggravation after putting up with Dad all those years."

Marge smiled. "I'm not supposed to tell you this. I promised Mom I wouldn't, but I think you should know. She cares a lot about you. I talk to her every now and then since you moved in with me, and she really wants to know how you're doing. Who do you think gave you all those maternity clothes?

Judy whined, "Well, you said some lady gave them to you at the bar."

"Yeah! That lady was Mom, and as you well know, she would not come in the bar. She would call and let me know she was dropping stuff off. Then she would leave everything in my car while I was working. Some of them were old things Mom had laying around. But for some of them, good ole Mom got out the sewing machine and made those things—just for you. She even left money in the glove box for us a couple of times."

"What?" A little tear drop rolled over Judy's long thick eyelashes.

Marge laughed as she grabbed a cookie.

"Marge, I'm so glad you told me. I thought the whole world was against me. I thought even my own mother didn't care about me."

"What do you mean?" Marge chided. "I'm nobody? I care! I love you!"

"Oh, Marge." Judy looked annoyed. "You know what I mean."

Then they both giggled.

After a few minutes of silence and watching the Christmas show on the television, Judy asked Marge, "Do you think Mom would come celebrate my birthday with us?"

"Probably! But that's over a month away. Let's get through Christmas first."

Judy wondered, "Are you going to tell Mom that you told me her secret about the clothes?"

"Probably," Marge yawned. "But why should it matter? At the moment I told you, it was the right thing to do. You needed to know she still cares."

"Marge, would you mind if I called Mom tomorrow and talked to her?"

Pausing for a few seconds, Marge leaned over toward Judy looking right in her eyes and said, "Why don't you call her now? Why wait until tomorrow if it would make you feel better? Just make sure you don't say a word about what happened in work today. I'm sure she'll hear about it sometime later. I just don't want to discuss it with her tonight."

"Oh, thank you!" Judy said as she dashed to the phone.

The minute her mother picked up the phone, Judy joyfully announced, "Hi, Mom. It's Judy."

"Judy, what a surprise! I was just praying about you and your sister. How are you doing, honey?"

"Better since Marge told me where she got the maternity clothes from."

Her mother gasped. "I told her not to tell you. But I guess I'm glad she did if it made you feel better."

"Hey, don't worry, Mom. I'm behaving. I guess I'm learning to be less ornery and more mature." She paused. "And I guess your prayers are working." Judy felt a little embarrassed with these admissions, but her longing for her mother overrode her embarrassment. "I'm getting welfare, food stamps, and Medicaid. So Marge and I are getting by okay. And the doctor says me and the baby are doing fine." She paused a few seconds, and then asked nervously, "How do you feel about being a grandmother?"

Her mother suppressed her tears. "I am very much looking forward to being a grandmother. And I'm so glad to hear that you, the baby, and Marge are all doing well."

Impulsively, Judy asked, "What are you doing for Christmas Eve and Christmas Day?"

"Are you inviting me over?" she wrinkled her eyebrows with anticipation.

"Sure, Mom! You can even stay overnight! Right, Marge?"

Stunned Marge replied, "Yeah. Sure!"

Then her mother said, "Judy, let me talk to your sister."

Marge walked over and took the phone with one eyebrow raised in wonderment. "Hi, Mom."

"Hi Marge. Did you hear what your sister just said?"

"Yes, I did." Marge quickly snapped to her senses. "It's fine by me if you want to come and stay overnight. You can sleep on my bed, and I'll sleep on the sofa."

"You don't have to do that, Marge. But I really would like to come and spend Christmas Eve and Christmas Day with you both. I was actually feeling kind of bad because I thought I would be spending Christmas all by myself."

Marge was quite taken back by such an admission from her mother. "You know, Mom, you're always welcome. In spite of all the things that have happened between us all, we both love you very much."

That was it. Her mother started softly crying into the phone. She couldn't hold back anymore and blubbered into the phone. "I'm so glad you invited me over for the Christmas holidays. That is such an answer to my prayers. It's so amazing that Judy called just as I was pouring my heart out to God over this."

Marge blinked back tears. "Mom, you should have said something sooner."

"I have to be sure it's your idea and not just another one of Judy's high-spirited outbursts. I wanted to be sure it was something that you wanted too," her mother said as she began to collect herself. "Thank you so much for the invitation. I'm so looking forward to it."

Marge was rather dumbfounded as she said, "We are too, Mom. We'll have a great Christmas together. We'll see you in a few days, Mom!"

After they hung up, Marge sat down in the kitchen chair next to the phone and was silent.

"Well, what did she say, Marge?" Judy finally asked.

"She said it sounded very good to her. She was feeling bad because she was afraid that this was going to be her first Christmas all alone, if we didn't ask her."

Judy apologized, "Marge, I'm so sorry if I put you on the spot. It just blurted out. I know we were talking about having her over for my birthday. But I just wanted to see her so much. I couldn't wait. I really wanted to see her before then. It just wouldn't be Christmas without her. And it sounded like she really wanted to be here with us, too! Don't you agree?"

"You know what? She told me you called her right while she was praying about being alone for Christmas. What a crazy coincidence!"

Marge quickly changed the subject and smiled. "After all the crazy stuff that went on in work today, this is a very welcomed thing! And yes, I agree. It feels good to know we will all still be together as a family for the holidays."

Judy chimed in with loud laughter. "After talking to Mom, it feels like life is going to be all right, robberies, pregnancies, and all. Don't you agree?"

Marge jokingly replied, "You with your stupid shenanigans! I just hope you don't make a habit of doing these kinds of whimsical things, or I'll be forced to kill you!"

Both girls rolled with laughter.

CHAPTER 10

Christmas Eve

Christmas Eve in 1973 fell on a Monday. Marge only worked a half a day and was off for Christmas because Buddy closed the bar for part of Christmas Eve and all of Christmas Day.

On Christmas Eve morning, Carla Brennan drove into town to pick up some grocery items at the big supermarket to bring with her for the two-day holiday at her daughters' home. As she walked through the store, she kept picking up items that looked appealing. As she pushed the shopping cart through the store, she prayed, "Oh, God, please bless this weekend for all three of us. Bless us to grow closer than we've ever been before. Bless us all to grow in your goodness, and bless us to remember all the good things you've done for us. Thanks so much for bringing us back together again."

It would have probably been a good idea for her to pray for wisdom with what she was dropping into her food cart. It was loaded with cakes, cookies, cheeses, nuts, and a canned ham. There was certainly much more food than they could possibly consume in two days.

As she drove to the girls' home, her heart was exhilarated with thoughts of spending the holiday with her two daughters in their own home. It could have been pouring rain and she would have still been full of joy at the thought of spending the Christmas holiday with them. But as luck would have it, snow was lightly flurrying. And even though it was not really sticking to the ground, it still added to the joy of the moment. By the time she reached her destination, the flurries stopped. But it didn't matter. Nothing could disappoint her.

She knocked on the front door to be welcomed first by Judy and the aroma of roast chicken from the kitchen.

"Hi, Mom!" Judy greeted her with a big hug and a kiss.

Carla was hoping her nervousness didn't show. She wanted this holiday to be a happy event for all three of them. "Hello, honey!" she said as she hugged and kissed Judy back.

Then it was Marge's turn. "Mom, I'm so glad you could be here."

"Me too!" her mother said as they hugged and kissed each other. "Boy, it smells good in here! What's cooking?"

"Roast chicken," Judy proudly stated.

"Well I'll be! You know how to roast a chicken?"

"Sure, Mom, it's not hard. You just put it in the oven and it cooks itself," Judy giggled as she took her mother's coat. "We are also having mashed potatoes, peas, sweet potatoes, and cranberry sauce."

"I didn't know you could do all that," her mother remarked.

"Well, Mom, they're instant mashed potatoes and everything else is canned."

"Oh!" her mother laughed. "What are you doing for gravy? Would you like me to show you how to make homemade gravy?"

"Sure!"

Before they could go any farther, Marge pointed to the Christmas tree and asked her mother what she thought of it.

"It's beautiful, Marge! What a nice job you did decorating your very own Christmas tree. I didn't get to see you last year for Christmas. Did you have a tree then too?"

Marge smiled apologetically, "Yes, I did and it was the same tree, and I'm so sorry we didn't get together last year. I'm so glad things are better between us, and you're getting to see it this year." She then showed her mother to her bedroom, took her purse, laid it on the bed, and ran out to the car to gather her mother's luggage.

As Marge was heading out the front door, she could hear her mother's voice trailing behind her, "Me too, Marge. I'm so glad."

When Marge returned, she remarked, "Marge, I would be very happy to sleep on the sofa. I really don't want to take your bed."

"Yeah, Mom, but my back is younger. Besides that, I insist." Then she giggled, "And by the way, what are you doing with all those groceries in your car?"

Her mother laughed right back at her, "I picked up a few things at the store this morning to bring with me for our holiday time together."

"What? You think we don't have any food?" Marge teased her.

The merry chit-chat went on right through dinner, until Carla innocently asked Marge how she was doing at work.

Marge's face drooped as she said, "I guess you heard."

"Heard what?"

"About the robbery."

"Robbery?" Her mother was dumbfounded.

Marge could tell she wasn't faking it by the look on her face. "Oh, I thought you must have heard about the robbery at Custer's. Seems like everyone else in town has been talking up a storm about it."

"No! I guess I've been too busy to keep up with the news. What happened? Did this happen while you were working?"

Marge told her mother the whole story while Judy cleared the dishes away. As she looked into her mother's face, she saw something in her mother that she never really understood before. Her mother wasn't getting all upset and losing her cool. It was certainly news that her mother did not want to hear. After all, this is serious when someone holds a gun to your daughter's head and threatens to blow her brains out. But her mother's face was strong and resolute like flint. Yet, it was soft and listening and caring. Marge was stricken with renewed realization of how strong her mother really was all those years when she was growing up. She was quite the opposite of the wimpy person that she had supposed her mother to be—one who helplessly stood by as her drunken husband behaved so badly. Marge suddenly had an even deeper awareness of the unusual character and strength that her mother possessed—of her wisdom, resoluteness, and endurance. She wondered how she didn't see this in her mother while she was growing up.

"You know, Marge," her mother commented, "please don't be upset with me for saying this. But when you go to places where trouble brews, you can expect to find trouble."

Marge unfortunately had to add one more quality to her mother's good attributes—honesty!

"I guess," Marge reluctantly replied. Her spirits began to dip again because she was remembering how much she was starting to hate her job. Plus the fact that she knew her mother didn't like those sorts of places and probably didn't want her working in such a place. Added to that were depression and remorse caused by all the terrible, painful memories the family went through with her father because of drinking at the bar. She wondered why she took a bar job to begin with. She started to mentally beat herself up with guilt.

Her mother softly continued, "We all know how booze makes people crazy. They not only lose all common sense, they lose all control of themselves, their lives, and everything else. And the really sad thing is that people don't need booze to mess up their lives. They can make enough of a mess out of their lives without getting drunk and out of control."

All Marge could do was sigh. She couldn't even answer her mother. She was right. Memories roamed through her mind of some of the messed up people and the messed up behavior that she saw at Custer's. These memories just added more bad memories on top of all the other miserable memories that she hated from the years of growing up with her drunken, abusive father.

Carla could see her daughter's discouragement and saw this as perhaps a good opportunity to try to steer her on to a better career path. "Marge, why don't you look for another job? You might not initially make as much money as you do at Custer's, but you could very possibly get a job that would make up the difference in pay with medical benefits, raises, and retirement, if you got into the right place. It shouldn't be that hard for you to find one. You did well in school, and that was while you were holding down that part-time job at the five and dime. Then you had that other job after you graduated running that deli for that nice Jewish man. You had a lot of responsibilities at that job. Remember? You had to take his deposits to the bank, get his mail, prep food, check in orders, and do a lot of legwork for him since he was wheelchair bound. Remember?"

"Yeah, I guess." Marge spirits began to rally up a little.

Her mother continued, "The best your job at Custer's could possibly offer is maybe you'd find a husband to get you out of there until he drinks himself to death. And what if you never get married? At very worst, you'll have a career of drinking yourself. No one can survive in an environment like that all their lives without somehow getting pulled into it to their own disadvantage. The Bible tells us that 'bad company corrupts good character.'"

Marge started to get a little annoyed now. Not only was her mother right, but now she was quoting the Bible again. When she was growing up, she heard her mother quote Bible verses quite often.

Carla sensed that is was time to back off. So she sat waiting with quiet anxiousness for Marge to process all that was just said.

Finally, Marge responded. "I guess you're right. I never drank before I started working at the bar. Maybe once in a while, I'd have a glass of wine or beer at a family event, but never enough to get buzzed. And lately, I've actually been drinking until I have a pretty good buzz. I've even been doing mixed drinks and shots. And you're right! I see some shameful stuff at the bar. It really makes me hate to be there sometimes. And this robbery! It's the icing on the cake." After a short pause, Marge continued, "But, Mom, I hate to say this. The Christmas holidays are not the time to go looking for a job. Maybe once New Year's Day is over, I'll start looking around."

Carla sighed in relief. "I think that sounds like a good idea, Marge."

Later that night, the three women sat snugly together on the sofa. They were like three little children laughing, eating cookies, and enjoying the Christmas shows on the television. Now seemed like a good time for Judy to ask the question that still wasn't completely resolved in her heart. Nervously she blurted out, "Mom, I know I asked this before. But are you really glad about being a grandmother?"

Her mother's eyebrows went up with astonishment. "Glad? Are you kidding? Don't you realize that baby is a gift from God? You've got to be kidding. I am very grateful for this wonderful gift. Why should you be so concerned?"

Now Judy was ready to ask the real question that was deeply burdening her heart. "Even though I got pregnant out of wedlock and the baby is illegitimate? I know you have to be disappointed that I didn't match up to your Christian standards."

Now Carla fully understood what was on her daughter's heart, she turned her face to lovingly look Judy in the eyes. "Judy, I forgive you, and I love you, and I always will. Okay, your behavior got you into some trouble, and you were doing things you shouldn't have been doing. But I still love you, and your baby is still my grandchild, isn't it?"

After a brief pause, her mother put her arm around her and softly said. "Oh honey! We all make mistakes, and we all need forgiveness. That's why God gave us a Savior. That's what Christmas is all about. Our Savior came into the world and took on flesh so we could be forgiven of our sins. And you're not the only one who needs forgiveness in life. We all do things that need God's forgiveness, myself included. And yet, He is so willing to give it to us. I think you also should be aware that God doesn't cares if the baby is illegitimate. He loves that baby regardless, and so do I."

She gave Judy a few seconds to think about what she just said. Then she went on. "Judy, I'm so pleased to see all the changes going on in you. Maybe having this baby is what was needed for you to calm down and learn some maturity. I've told you many times that God has a good purpose in everything. He even brings good things out of our mistakes—even unexpected pregnancies. Isn't that wonderful? By the way, I brought some Christmas gifts for my grandchild. I can't wait until tomorrow morning for you to open them."

"Really, Mom?" Judy flung her arms around her mother in great relief. "I was so afraid you would hold it against me about the baby being born out of wedlock and be mad at me for the rest of my life for going against what you believe in like I did. I love you."

Judy was finally at peace in her heart now that she knew that her mother forgave her and that she had the confirmation that God did not hold her bad choices against her or her baby. Life was suddenly so good. She felt restored in her relationship with her mother and hopeful for herself and her baby to have acceptance in the world and a good life ahead. The future was finally looking promising.

All three women laughed joyously. And the rest of their Christmas Eve and Christmas Day holiday was a wonderful time of warm, family bonding for all three of them.

CHAPTER II

The Offer

During the week after New Year's Day, Marge was at work talking to a few customers, one of whom happened to be Joe Veroni, the broker and owner of a local insurance agency. It was lunchtime and the customers were enjoying all the small talk and joking around. Joe was fascinated with Marge's account of the robbery.

"I'll bet you were really scared," he said.

Marge's eyebrows shot up. "You bet your booties I was."

"I'm surprised you didn't quit your job," Joe replied looking sideways at Marge as he took a sip from his drink.

"Hm-m!" Marge seemed to be keeping her thoughts to herself, except for the sly return look to Joe that betrayed what was really going on in her head.

Joe gave her a nod and a comprehending smile. "I guess you need to be working so you can pay your bills, right?"

"You could say that." Marge was being cautious as she thought to herself, *What's this guy up to?* She steered away from him as she starting cleaning up the bar after the customers who had just finished their lunches and were getting ready to leave. After she finished picking up all her tips and rinsing all the glasses, she went back over to Joe to see if he wanted another drink.

Being careful so that Marge would not be suspicious of him, he asked as calmly as he could, "So, have you been looking?"

Marge was felt rather defensive in spite of his efforts. "Why do you ask?"

Joe chuckled at Marge's directness. "You know a guy named Bill Bach?" he asked in a low voice.

"Yeah?" Marge was still trying to figure him out and was now suspicious because he mentioned Bill's name.

"Well, he's a good friend of mine."

"Yeah?" Marge's curiosity was piqued now.

"He's been seeing your mother since she's been widowed, right?"

"Yeah?" Marge replied suspiciously. She still found it difficult to trust Bill Bach because of how soon after her father died he started *making moves* on her mother, but she was trying to be graceful about it.

"Well, Bill and I have been friends for quite a few years now, and I was having a conversation with him about how we really need some good help in our office, but I haven't had time to run an ad, and start looking, and do all that interviewing for someone. My claims adjustor really needs someone to help him out. He's up to his neck in paperwork, and he needs someone who is hard working, responsible, and intelligent enough to learn the business to help him keep it all in order. Maybe even help him run the department."

"Are you thinking of me?" Marge was catching on quickly. Joe was either doing Bill a favor, who in turn was trying to use his influence to please her mother, or else her mother asked Bill for a favor in helping to find a job for her. Either way, Marge was open to taking advantage of a possibly good opportunity for starting a better career than the one she had at Custer's.

"I really like how right to the point you are," Joe stated. "And yes! As soon as Bill told me about you and how your mother would like you to leave this job and start something better, I was interested in talking to you. Although I haven't known you personally, I've known about you from visiting from time to time here at Custer's. I can see that you are quite a smart girl and a very hard worker. I think you'd be perfect for this job. That is, if it is something you think you'd like to do."

"Oh-h-h-h!" Marge understood perfectly now. Her mother's influence was definitely behind all this, but she didn't directly solicit Joe for a job on her behalf. So Marge wasn't quite so put off by Joe's proposal. Joe really did need someone, and it really could be a unique opportunity. Now Marge wanted to find out more. "I'd love to, but I don't know first base from outfield when it comes to …" she paused, "insurance or claims adjusting."

"Marge, believe me. It does not take a rocket scientist. Just reasonable intelligence and hard work. You are certainly intelligent enough. And you are certainly capable of doing the work. Plus, I just know you will put into the work the effort needed to do the job well. Listen. Right now, I've got a few bompies in there that I wonder why I've got them working for me. They seem to think coffee breaks should last the better part of the day. I'm betting you would work circles around them."

Marge laughed because she knew some of the people he was talking about. She was also amused that he called them bompies. She *thought what an unusual word selection but it fit so well.* They sometimes came in for lunch. She was sure Joe was just joking, and that they weren't as bad as he was saying. But she also knew they weren't especially ambitious types because of some of their behavior and the conversations she overheard from them in the bar.

Joe continued, "If you decide to give it a try, I'll make sure you get the training not only to do the job, but I'll even help you to advance into a lifetime career. I promise you. I'll help you each step of the way for reaching your career goals too."

Marge was seriously contemplating the offer. So now she was wondering what this would mean for her financially. "How much would you be paying me?"

"How much do you make here at Custer's?"

"Well, it depends on business. On an average week, I clear around $175 with tips and base pay. Base pay is very minimal. During the holidays, I really rake it in. So far for this Christmas holiday, I've been bringing home closer to $250, not including base pay."

In 1973, that was a lot of money. "Gee!" Joe looked surprised. "You are not going to start out at that type of pay in any job that is respectable. Not that you couldn't work your way up to it. Especially in the insurance business. If you decided to be an agent, you could very well double that in only a few years. It would probably be a little bit of a financial adjustment for you to start out though."

"Yes, I know," Marge coolly replied.

Joe smiled. He could see that she was interested in what he had to offer and was ready to make a career change. "Listen, I can't match your income to start you out, but after thirty days, you'll have medical insurance, life insurance, paid holidays, paid vacation, paid personal days, and after one year of employment, we'll start you on a retirement fund. I don't know if you know how much of a difference that makes, but it makes a significant difference, especially over time."

"Uh-huh!" The retirement fund didn't mean too much to Marge at her young age. However, she was impressed with all the other benefits. Being smart enough not to look too anxious, she gazed directly into his eyes, and asked, "So what will you be paying me?"

Joe continued, "I'll be stretching my neck, so I don't want you to say anything to anyone else. You got that? I mean no one!"

"Okay." Marge still remained cool.

"I'll start you out at $120 per week with a $10 per week increase for each month for the next three months."

"A hundred and fifty dollars per week after three months?" Marge bit her lip thinking.

"Yeah. Plus all those benefits after thirty days. What do you think?"

Marge was enticed. Even though she was making more in the bar, she didn't have all those benefits. Nor did she get paid vacations. The type of work sounded rather interesting, certainly better than being at Custer's with the drunks, the fights, and the robbery. And now that Judy had her welfare checks coming in, she could manage for a few months on less money. She could see her name plate on her desk with a title, Claims Adjuster Assistant, or maybe Insurance Agent. If this guy was true to his word, she would surpass her weekly barmaid income in a few years anyway. But a momentary surge of fear came over her and she blurted out, "What if I take the job and find out I don't like it?"

"Why don't you take a morning off from Custer's and come into the office and see what you think."

"What if a few years from now, I'm not advancing like I would like to be? Please forgive me if I sound insulting, but how can I be sure you aren't just making promises to do Bill and Mom a favor?"

Marge's bold challenge startled him. He sighed with frustration, "Well, Marge, I don't know what to say to you. Maybe you need to go talk to Bill and your mother."

"I really don't know Bill personally. He's just the guy dating my mother."

Joe politely gave up with a smile. "He's a really great guy. It's a shame you don't." He put his business card down on the bar, took one last sip of his drink, and then started to leave.

"Wait a minute," Marge shouted. "I'm sorry. Can we make an appointment for me to come out to see you next Wednesday morning?"

He turned around to look back at her with an amused smile on his face. "How about Tuesday morning? I've got appointments with clients on Wednesday. Tuesday would be much better for me."

"Great!" Marge grinned. "I'll see you Tuesday morning!"

"Good!" Joe laughed and shook his head with wonder. "Be there at 9:00 a.m."

"Terrific! I'll be there!" Marge hollered after him as he walked out the door, "Bye! Hey, thanks a lot!"

CHAPTER 12

Checking It Out

The following Tuesday morning, Marge called Buddy and told him she wasn't feeling well and needed to stay home from work. She knew she was lying, but she certainly didn't want to tell him the truth. On her way to the insurance office, she worried that someone would see her or her car at the insurance office and tell Buddy. She knew there was a very good chance of getting caught in her lie because the Veroni Insurance Agency office building was only three blocks away from the bar. But she was willing to take the chance.

She made great effort to be punctual. And in her attempt to look businesslike, she wore a straight gray wool skirt and a matching jacket with a black turtleneck sweater underneath. As she got out of the car, she checked her stockings for one last time to make sure there were no runs in them. Then she took one last deep breath and headed toward the office door.

Joe Veroni was busy in his office, so his secretary smiled and instructed Marge to have a seat and fill out an application. Although Marge thought it was a little presumptuous to give her the application form as she hadn't yet committed to applying for the job, she did like the formality and business atmosphere of the office and reception area. She thought to herself, *Hot dog! I like it here. This is for me.*

When she finished filling out her application, she handed it back to the secretary, who asked her to be seated again until Joe finished with his call. It was only a matter of minutes before Joe hung up the phone and the secretary called Marge to go in and see him. The minute he saw her, he stood up to greet her. As they shook hands, he said, "Well, Marge, I'm so impressed. You really look like a businesswoman today. What a big difference from the pretty young woman I saw in the bar last week. Have a seat so we can talk a little."

The secretary handed Joe the application and gestured Marge to the seat in front of Joe's desk. Joe and Marge both sat down. Then Joe began to review Marge's application. He asked her a few questions about her responsibilities and the work she did at the five and dime store and the deli job that she did previous to her job at Custer's. Then he asked her what she thought of the office.

"Well, I really like the atmosphere of being in the office. But if I could see what it is like to do the work that you do here, I would probably know better how I really would like doing this type of work."

Joe shrugged. "That's a good idea." He seemed like he was a little pressed for time, but he was willing to do what was needed to help Marge get comfortable and to make up her mind. He led her into the claims adjustments office and introduced her to the employees there. There was an older man, who seemed to be the manager of that group; a younger man in his late twenties; and two young women around her age. As Marge entered the room, she wondered if she made a mistake. What if these three come into Custer's and say something so Buddy finds out? *Oh well! Too late*, she thought to herself.

"Hi everyone! I want you to meet Marge," Joe said as he showed Marge through the door.

"Hi! Don't I know you from Custer's?" one of the young women said.

Joe immediately sensed Marge's concern and quickly answered, "Marge was thinking of taking the open position, but she wanted to see what it was like to work here before she made any firm commitments. It does not necessarily mean she will take the job, and you are not to talk about it outside of work."

Marge gave him a look to let him know that she was relieved by him saying that.

The older man in the department extended his hand for a handshake. "Glad to meet you, Marge! I'm Bob Barnhardt, the manager of the claims department! Come on in."

Joe let Bob know he was leaving Marge with him. "I've got some things I need to do back in my office. When you're done showing Marge around and explaining the work to her, please bring her back over to my office to finish talking to me, okay?"

"No problem!" Bob said as Joe was leaving the room.

In the meantime, Marge was noticing the name plates on everyone's desks as she was scoping out the office. She felt a little excited about the atmosphere of the office and the prospects of having her own desk with a name plate on it.

"Can you type, Marge?" Bob inquired.

"Oh, boy. I had typing in high school, and I could type about thirty-five words a minute back then. But it's been a little while. I don't really know how well I can type now, but I'm sure it wouldn't take long to get back up to speed. I hope this job would not be all typing."

"Not really. But it would help if you can type. Carl types by the two-fingered hunt-and-peck method, and he gets by all right," Bob said as he pointed to the younger gentleman.

"Oh," Marge said with a puzzled look on her face.

Bob reassured her, "I'm sure that if you could type before, it won't take long for you to pick it back up again. Truthfully, I would prefer that you could type better than Carl, as it would certainly help with getting work done faster."

Carl chuckled as he resumed his work.

Bob continued. "This job isn't all just sitting around in the office anyway. After you've been here in the office a few weeks and you've learned all the procedures in the office, you'll go out into the field with someone for a while, probably me, and learn how to fill out claims reports and assess damages for actual insurance claims."

"Wow!" Marge raised both eyebrows with interest. Already the job sounded more interesting. "How will I know the value of the vehicle I'm appraising, or the actual extent of the damages?"

"You might not be going out to assess damages to a car. You might be going out to assess the damages to someone's home. You also need to know that an insurance adjuster does more than just assess the value of something and the damages done to it. An adjuster also has to be a bit of a detective and investigate the claims, negotiate with the property owner and repairman for settlements, and then authorize a payment to the claimant on behalf of the insurance company on the policy. There is a lot to learn. But it is good work, and it's very interesting work, if you don't mind working and like to use your head. I will certainly be overseeing everything you do until you're competent enough to work on your own."

Marge's excitement was starting to peak. This really sounded challenging and very interesting, much more interesting than just serving drinks and sandwiches in a bar. "Are there special classes? Do I need to get certified?"

"No, not really. New Jersey doesn't require licensure for insurance adjusters. However, to be a sales agent, you would need a license. I would suggest just taking this job one step at a time and learning what you can as you go. I think you will find insurance claims adjusting very interesting and satisfying as a career." Bob seemed to pull back in hesitation. "That is, if you decide this is what you want to do."

Marge was taken back a little bit by the hesitation. "Of course I want to. Why wouldn't I?"

Bob looked intently at her and stated, "Some days I get a little discouraged. It seems like whenever people come in here looking for a job, they appear very enthusiastic. Then once they have the job, the honeymoon is over. After that, they seem to lose their ambition and not take their work so seriously."

Now Marge felt uneasy. "Oh," she said as she looked around the room to see how the three others reacted to Bob's statement. One girl shrugged. The other girl rolled her eyes in her head and looked away. And Carl just looked away.

Bob signaled to Marge to follow him. As they headed down the hallway to Joe's office, he said "Don't get me wrong. These are all nice young people working with me. But they don't know how to work. I don't know what Joe might have said to you, but I need someone who is willing to apply his- or herself to this work. It's not just pushing papers around and filling out forms. You've got to be a go-getter. You've got to be willing to apply your noodle to what you're doing. They don't really seem to know how to do that. However, they're all good at having parties on the weekend. And I don't like it when they go out to lunch and have a drink with their food because then they come back all lethargic. I'm hoping we can find someone who is ambitious and willing to put real effort into the work."

Marge giggled as she remembered what Joe said about them all being bompies. She was beginning to see that both Joe and Bob were really genuine people who truly just needed some better help. Then she thought to herself, *Why don't they just demand that these three get their acts together and get serious about their work? After all, what are they being paid for?* Then after she thought about it some more, it dawned on her that it's kind of like the people in the bar. You can't make them change. They've got to want to make the changes.

When Marge got back to Joe's office, Joe filled her in on the actual situation in the claims adjustment office. "Bob is a real ace as a claims adjuster. He knows his job extremely well. He knows how to get to the bottom of an investigation. He's good at negotiating a good deal between the claimant and the repair people. He's great with details. He's organized and a hard worker. And he makes the insurance carrier that our agency represents happy. However, he is not a pusher, and the kids he has working for him right now are just that—kids! You've got to stand behind them and monitor everything they do. We need to find someone who is motivated and mature. Someone who is a go-getter and doesn't need someone standing behind them all the time to make sure they're doing the job right. From what I know already about you, I'm betting that you are just that kind of person. Someone who works hard, and applies herself, and doesn't need pushing. As far as Bob goes, I really can't replace him. He is my best and only good claims adjuster. Besides that, I really like the guy. I think you'll find him very good to work with. As for those other three," Joe waved his hand in disgust, "I guess eventually we'll replace them."

Marge was a little taken back by Joe's candor, but she understood as she smiled and nodded with agreement.

"Well, do you want the job?"

"I sure do!" Marge said with a sparkle.

Joe gave a sigh of relief. "Wonderful! When do you want to start?"

"Well, Buddy's been very good to me." Cautiously, she went on, "Almost like family. He knew my dad before he died. So he treated me almost like a daughter. I really do have to give him time to replace me."

Joe nodded in approval. "Well, how long do you think that will take?"

"I'm not sure. But it will take him at least a week to find someone and another week to train them."

"So you think about two weeks?"

"At least two, maybe more." Marge saw Joe knit his eyebrows. "But probably only two. Who knows? Maybe even less," she recanted.

Looking at his calendar book, he said "Okay. Let's say then that you will be starting by the first Monday in February at the latest."

Marge looked over the desk at his calendar and confirmed. "Right! If I can start sooner, would you like me to start sooner?"

Joe looked over his glasses at her. "Sure! The sooner we can get you trained and helping Bob, the better."

Marge stood up extending her hand like a true businesswoman and said,

"Thanks so much for your time this morning. I'm looking forward to working with you."

Joe smiled at her professional demeanor and returned the handshake. "Likewise! We're looking forward to bringing you on board."

Marge stepped out of the office door into the sunshine feeling exhilarated, telling herself, *New beginnings; new job; a new stand on life. Wow!* She giggled as she walked to her car, "No more fights or dealing with drunks and other undesirable characters at Custer's. This is my *last stand* at Custer's and a new stand on life. I'm done working with all those messed up people at the bar. I'm done with being around the booze and all the problems it brings."

CHAPTER 13

Parting Ways

The following morning, Marge sat at breakfast with her traditional cup of instant coffee. The sun was dancing brightly on the kitchen table. Marge's spirits were also brightly dancing. She chuckled as she told Judy, "Mom was so happy when I told her I was taking the job at Veroni's Insurance, but I'm very sure she wasn't surprised because she probably already heard the news through Bill."

Judy was busy making herself scrambled eggs as the two girls shared their enthusiasm over the good news. "Are you nervous about telling Buddy today?"

"A little. You know Buddy has been very good to me."

"Uh-huh," Judy said as she popped her bread into the toaster.

"I'm sure he won't have any trouble finding someone else though. The money at Custer's is good, and there's always someone looking for a job that pays so good. I'm betting that he wouldn't even have to advertise. With just word of mouth, I'm sure he would find someone to take my place."

"You're probably right," Judy replied as she preoccupied herself with setting her place at the table, along with salt and pepper and a glass of milk.

"You know, as much as I was getting sick of that place, I'm really going to miss some of those people, especially the old-timers."

Judy stopped to look at Marge in amazement. "Really?" She obviously could not understand.

Amused at the puzzled look on Judy's face, Marge went on. "You get to know the people, and some of them become friends. You do get attached to them—even if they are a little messed up."

"Well, just remind yourself about that guy holding that gun to your head, if you start getting too sentimental and want to change your mind," Judy scolded her.

Marge let loose a belly laugh. "Don't worry, Mom! I'm looking too forward to the new job to change my mind."

"Mom!" Judy retorted in an accusatory manner. "You called me Mom? You've got nerve." But Judy actually enjoyed her sister's joking with her.

Both girls looked at each other and burst out laughing.

Marge looked at the clock, "Oh dear! I guess I better get going!" She gulped her last few drops of coffee and quickly placed her empty cup in the sink. The girls said their good-byes as Marge slipped out the door with her feet barely touching the ground.

The first thing Marge did as she walked into the bar was to look for Buddy. "Buddy? I need to talk to you." There was no answer, so she hollered down the basement to where all the beer kegs were. "Buddy!" she hollered again.

"Yeah! Just a minute! I'll be right up."

The old-timers were already there having their morning social time and beer. So Marge checked all their glasses. When Buddy arrived back upstairs, Marge asked him if she could speak to him in the kitchen for a minute. When she told him the news that she had another job and was giving him her two weeks' notice, he didn't seem at all upset. In fact, he seemed sort of relieved and rather happy for her. Marge was a little disappointed that Buddy wasn't at least a little sad over her announcement, but she was comforted because she didn't want him to feel bad.

Later on at the bar, after Marge told some of her customer friends about the news, old Jesse told her, "You know, ever since the robbery, I think Buddy regretted having a woman behind the bar by herself like that, even though having a pretty girl like you there has drawn in a lot of business. He said something to us about how concerned he was about leaving you there after that robbery."

Marge felt good to think that people cared so much about her. But she was still looking forward to moving on to the next phase in her life.

In less than a week, Buddy found the person to take Marge's place. In fact, he hired two people. Much to everyone's amazement, he hired a man to stay behind the bar for the full dayshift, and he also hired an attractive woman to help out just at lunchtime to continue to draw the lunch crowd in.

"Boy! Is that Buddy a shrewd one," Pops laughed when he heard the news.

"Yeah! I guess we don't have to find another hangout," Jesse pitched in. He paused quickly. "But you know we'll always love you, Margie!" he crooned at her.

Marge laughed until tears came to her eyes.

When Buddy entered the bar, Marge teased him. "Gee, Buddy! I must be pretty good if it takes two people to replace me."

Buddy laughed. "Yeah, well, we'll miss you Marge. I hope you understand me bringing in two. I think it will be good to have a woman here at lunchtime. But I really wanted to have a man behind the bar. I just feel better about having a man behind the bar, especially after that robbery."

Marge sympathetically replied, "I really do understand!"

Buddy went on, "The other thing is lunches are crazy in here anyway, and I'm getting too old to kill myself like that anymore. The more help at lunch time the better, right?"

"Yeah," Jesse chimed in, "he's got to save himself for his pretty wife."

Buddy chuckled at Jesse's silly remark. "I guess I do. I really only plan to keep on working like this for a few more years. Then I want to retire. If I have myself a heart attack, it'll spoil my plans."

They all laughed.

The following week, which was Marge's last week at work, was a very easy week. Marge did practically no work except for showing the two new people where everything was, the daily routines, and how the customers were used to having everything done. By the end of Wednesday, Buddy told Marge if she was anxious to start her new job, she could let her new boss know and perhaps start a few days early. But if she wanted to stay, it was no problem. She could stay for the rest of the week. "It's up to you," Buddy told her.

Marge thought about it for a few seconds. She was not only getting pretty bored, but she had to split the tips with the two others. "You know what, Buddy? If I don't take a vacation now, I won't get one until I have a year in my new job. Maybe I'll just take the next two days off."

Buddy reached into the register and pulled out three twenties from under the tray. "Here! I know it won't make up for your tips, but it's something to help cover you for the next couple of days anyway."

Tears rimmed around Marge's eyes as she hugged Buddy good-bye. "Buddy, it's really been great working for you."

When she finished hugging Buddy, she noticed Jesse, Pops, and Art making fun of her, laughing, looking at each other, and shrugging.

"You can always come back and say *hi* once in a while," Pops teased her.

"Yeah! And what about me?" Jesse whined. "You didn't give me a good-bye hug, and I tell you I love you more than anybody in the place."

Laughing heartily, Marge walked out from behind the bar and hugged her three old-timer buddies good-bye. "Oh! Don't you worry, I'll be back, and I'll make you buy me a drink and a sandwich too."

With that, they all laughed, and Marge took her purse from under the register and left. When she got in her car, reality struck. She realized that even though she genuinely loved some of the people there, she would not ever be coming back again. She would miss them, especially the old-timers. But she really didn't want anything to do with the bar life or any of its problems anymore. Remorsefully, she thought out loud, "Mom was right; this is not really a good place to be." She started her car, and as she drove off, she said, "Good-bye Custer's!" She was truly done with that chapter of her life.

CHAPTER 14

Bright New Beginnings

Marge's first day at work was a snowy morning. There were about four inches of snow on the ground, and the sun was shining so brightly that between the snow and the sun, it was blinding. Marge scraped the snow off her windshield as she anticipated all the excitement of her new job.

Right from the beginning, Marge and Bob hit it off. Marge paid close attention to everything that Bob told her, and she learned the job very quickly. She put great enthusiasm into all that she did.

She was aware the other employees resented her by the glances they exchanged every time she passed their desks. Marge decided to ignore them. But one day, Rosemary, the girl who liked to sarcastically roll her eyes at people, was showing Marge how to look up a depreciation rate on an automobile. When Marge caught on with her usual enthusiasm, Rosemary barked at her, "Relax! Do you always have to be such a showoff?" Then Carl and Marsha, the other two claims adjusters, both chuckled jealously.

This time their behavior was hard to ignore, and Marge did feel a little hurt. But Marge decided to remain oblivious to their behavior. She kept reminding herself of Joe and Bob's promises that she would do well in her new career if she worked at it and did a good job. With that, Marge decided she wasn't there to win a popularity contest. So after a while, the other employees could see that their opinions did not affect her excellent performance. She continued to learn and improve her skills daily. So they just stayed away from her. *That's fine by me,* Marge would think to herself. *Who wants to pay the price it would take to be a friend with someone like you?*

A little while after, Bob was going over the procedures with Marge for payment on a hospital bill from a client's auto accident. When they were out of the earshot of the other three people, Bob commented to Marge, "You really impress me, Marge! You're very focused on your work, and you've got a mind of your own. I must say, you're very smart not to let those other three get to you or distract you from doing your work. You've taken a good stand with them, and that shows that you've got a good business head. Just be sure to stay smart and keep doing a good job without offending anyone, if possible, unless you have to. And guaranteed you'll go a long way in life and in your career."

Marge was bursting with pride as she grinned at him. Bob's words were of great encouragement to her. She was really enjoying her new job and was very motivated by the great future of her new career move. She found great pleasure in all the things she was learning and found an immense sense of achievement with all the challenges she faced. Plus, she loved working with Bob. He was a great teacher and job coach.

Early the next week, Marge received a call from Judy at work. "Hi, Marge! I hope you don't mind me calling you at work, but I just really had to tell you. You won't believe this, but I'm rolling in the money now. Not only did I get my welfare check last week, but today I went out to get the mail, and Mom and Bill just sent me a birthday card with fifty dollars in it."

"Wow!" Marge choked. "That's great! Now you can take me out to dinner."

Judy laughed, "That sounds like a great idea. I don't feel like cooking anyway. Want me to come out and meet you at work?"

"Okay. Sure!" Marge chuckled with amusement at Judy's willingness to meet her at work and buy dinner. It was only a couple of months ago when Judy didn't even want to live, let alone be seen in public. It was as if the healing of her relationship with her mother, plus all the encouragement she was receiving from her mother and sister, accompanied by the joyful anticipation they all had about the expected baby, gave Judy the healing and encouragement that she needed. She displayed a strong recovery from her depression and was fully ready to enjoy life again.

"So, where would you like to go?" Judy joyfully asked.

Marge didn't want to dampen the joy of the moment, but she was anxious to get back to her paperwork. So she suggested, "Let's figure that out when you get here. There are a few places nearby that aren't too expensive. Come meet me at the office around 4:30, and we will decide then."

After she hung up the phone, Marge sat still for a minute to think about Mom and Bill's joint gift. She wasn't sure if she was comfortable with it or not. Marge wanted good things for her mother, and Bill seemed like an okay guy. However, Marge was still rather unsettled about how Bill was becoming so involved with not only her mother, but now with the rest of the family. For the time being, she decided to push those concerns aside because at this point in time she had work to do, and everything in life seemed to be taking a turn for the better for her sister and for herself. It was so good to see Judy's spirits so greatly improved. And instead of hearing her moan about how she ruined two lives, Judy had a completely new outlook full of joyful expectation with the baby on the way. Besides that, Marge's life was now also heading in a much better direction. With all these wonderful turnarounds, life had become good for the both of them.

CHAPTER 15

Reality Hits Home

That same week, Danny was standing in the Schisler kitchen as he opened up a piece of mail from welfare. It was a notice that he would have to pay a certain amount of money to the welfare office that would in turn apply his payment to support his child and the child's mother.

Danny's hand trembled as he read the letter. Finally, he blew up into a rage. On hearing the commotion, his father came running out to the kitchen exclaiming, "What in the world is the matter with you?"

"That stupid girl turned me in to the welfare department, and now they're trying to make me pay for her support."

"Son! What are you talking about? Explain!"

"Judy Brennan," Danny scowled at his father. Expecting a serious reprimand from his father, Danny went on, "I got her pregnant, and she must have told the welfare office because now they want me to pay support for her."

Ed's mouth dropped open. "You mean Joe Brennan's daughter?" He paused. "I'm going to be a grandfather?" He wasn't even concerned about Danny's dilemma, nor about his son's lack of morality. He was just pleased to hear he was going to be a grandfather. "Why didn't you tell me?"

"Dad! You're happy?" Dan was shocked. "How did your thinking get so messed up? Are you some kind of a hippie?"

Ed pulled out a chair and told his son to sit down while he finished buttoning his shirt. "Let's talk, son."

Dan reluctantly sat down and pushed out another chair with his foot for his father to sit down next to him.

Ed obligingly sat down and continued. "I don't need to remind you, son, it's just you and me. Not that it is such a bad thing, but I would love it to be more. A grandchild and a daughter-in-law to join us would be so wonderful."

"Dad! A daughter-in-law? A baby? Are you crazy?" Danny was incredulous.

Ed tried to be dignified. "Well yes! Our lives would be so much richer with these additions to our family. With just the two of us, life can get very lonely."

Danny got up to walk away, and his father also stood up and started bellowing as he followed after him, "You listen to me! You don't know what you're throwing away. Not only is that a real child, it's your child! It's my grandchild! How could you? How many times have I told you how lonely it was for me being raised in an orphanage and having your mother die with all of her family being over in England? There's no one here but us two. If anything happens to either one of us, we're all alone in this world. There is no other family who is really here for us, except for maybe a few good friends. And even at that, during the holidays, they've got their own families. They don't think about people like us who are all alone for the holidays."

Dan's head dropped. He remembered many a Christmas with a very depressed father looking at the tree with all the gifts under it and feeling the great emptiness. He could never wait for Christmas morning to be over so he could go out and do something just to get away from all the oppressive emptiness of Christmas morning with a downhearted father.

Ed continued, "Stop walking away and look at me."

Danny reluctantly stopped and faced his father.

Ed continued, "I did the best I could by myself, but it was very hard for me. Who do you suppose I talked to before you started talking? Who would be here for you if I died? Maybe you would like to just drink yourself unconscious every time you started to feel bad, like I do."

Ed was looking Dan straight in the eye as he was yelling. But when the tears welled up in his eyes, he started to blubber and looked away from his son.

Danny saw his father plenty of times in a sullen, gloomy mood, but he rarely saw his father cry. He quietly walked away and left the house. He learned from past experience, this was the best thing to do when Dad got carried away. Just leave. After standing on the front walk for a minute, he decided to go for a ride on his bike and think about things. His driving was aggressive. And the cold winter air made his face sting with frost. After a half hour of wandering aimlessly, he decided to return home. He had chest pains from the guilt he felt for leaving his father sobbing and alone like he did. He was also guilt stricken by his father's statement about throwing his grandchild away. Danny really loved his father, but he sometimes found his father's profound gloominess very difficult to live with. And his father's behavior wasn't helping him with his own stresses over his situation with Judy and the welfare office.

Before he went back into the house, he paused to collect his thoughts. As he regained his composure, he stopped thinking about himself and started thinking about how much worse he must have made his father feel by leaving the way he did.

"Dad," he called as he walked back into the house. His father had returned to the kitchen and was sitting at the table with his back leaned up against the wall and his foot propped on the chair next to him. A long silence followed until Ed threw his empty beer can into the trash bag and headed to the refrigerator for more.

"I'm sorry if I upset you, son." Ed seemed to be much calmer now. "You have to make your own choices." He got out two more cans of beer and handed one to Danny.

They both sat at the table and opened their beers. A short silence followed, and then Danny spoke up. "I took a little ride to clear my head, Dad. I hope you didn't feel bad when I left."

Ed quietly shook his head no.

"I know you feel lonely sometimes." He started to choke a little. Then he collected himself and went on. "I love you very much, Dad. And I want you to be happy. But I don't want to give up my life. I enjoy being free and doing what I want to do. I'm not ready to be tied down to a wife and a kid. I really want my freedom. It's not that I don't care about you or the baby or Judy." He faked a smile. "I'm just not done playing the field. It's too much fun meeting the other girls and hanging out with my friends. I hope you understand. But I need to make my own decisions on what's right for me."

Toying with the beer can in his hand, Ed turned over his thoughts and his feelings, trying to put his own desires aside and allow his son to make his own choices. "Then this is what you should have. You're too old for me to be steering your ship for you anymore. You are a man now."

Danny was amused with his father calling him a man. He still sometimes felt like a kid in a man's world. "Dad, I may be a man, but I'm sorry. I'm really not ready to marry or have a kid. Maybe a few years from now I will find a wife and marry her. Then you'll have your grandchildren that you want so much."

His father's voice was low and soft. "In the meantime, how many other women will there be who will be taking care of my grandchildren that I will never know about?"

These words struck Danny hard. He not only realized that his father still disapproved of his life choices, but as his father said, he could leave a trail of illegitimate children behind. Guilt started to set in. Maybe they would have lives of depression like his father had because of being abandoned and lonely.

Thoughtfully pouring a few cool gulps of beer down his throat, Danny's anger over welfare and Judy had temporarily diminished. His mind switched to new thoughts. He remembered what his father said before about drinking himself to death every time he started to feel bad, and it caused Dan to worry. The reality occurred to him that maybe his father had some serious problems going on with both depression and drinking. Embarrassing and distressing memories replayed in Danny's head. He remembered those times he had to retrieve his vomiting father from the bar. And other times when he had to keep his father from arguing, even fighting with people because he was too drunk to be reasonable. The more frightening part was that these kinds of incidences were happening more and more frequently.

Danny was just about to talk to his father about his drinking when he spoke up in a very surly voice, "Suppose you do wait a few years to have your family, and I'm not even alive anymore?"

Danny knew he was not going to get anywhere with his father in his present state. This was Danny's cue to keep his mouth shut. His father was drinking and upset. This was no mixture to tangle with. The conversation was ended. It was time for Dan to go meet his friends at Custer's.

CHAPTER 16

The following day during the morning coffee break at work, Danny called the welfare office from the company's office phone while all the office girls were still in the break room. "Hi, I received a notice to start making support payments for this baby and its mother, both of whom I have nothing to do with. Who am I supposed to talk to?"

"Can I have your name?" the nasal voice inquired.

"Schisler, Dan Schisler."

"And may I have the name of the party you are being required to support?"

"Judy Brennan! And I'm not supporting her if I can help it."

"I see. Just a minute while I pull the file."

Waiting was difficult because he was angry and also quite anxious to be done with the phone call before one of the office girls returned. He bounced his leg up and down as if all his bouncing would make things go faster.

Finally the women returned to the phone saying, "Yes, and what did you want to know?"

"Why do I have to pay for her?" Danny impatiently replied.

"Because she says you're the father."

"That …" Danny stopped himself. "I have nothing to do with this girl or her baby. It's her word against mine, and I'm not paying."

The voice on the phone answered with practiced coolness, "Sir, if you insist on not paying, we'll have to issue a summons to have a blood test done on you once the baby is born. If it shows positive evidence that you are the baby's father, we'll have to summon you to court, and most likely we will attach your wage, and not only will you be making monthly payments, but you will be making back payments for all the months the mother was pregnant and collecting welfare money before the baby was born. However, if it's not your baby, as you say, you will have nothing to worry about."

"Attach my wage? What does that mean?"

"Sir, that means an automatic deduction will be made from your paycheck before you receive your weekly pay."

Danny gulped incredulously. "Are you kidding?"

The voice continued, "Were you or are you married to this girl?"

"No!" shot Danny as he thought to himself, *What a stupid question*!

"Well, since you are not married, unless you admit that you were the father, you would not be held responsible. But since she is saying that you are the father, the next step would be to wait for the baby to be born and for the welfare office to summon you to get the blood test—that is unless you admit it's your child and start making payments before then. Again, I would like to remind you that if you are proven to be the father, you will owe back support for all the months that she carried the baby and was collecting welfare money. Would you like to make the arrangements to start making payments now?"

"No!" Danny abruptly answered. "And when does she say this baby is due?"

"I don't have that information. But she has been receiving welfare since October."

Danny was afraid he was licked. He was certain that a blood test would prove the baby was his, but he still would not own up to anything. If there was even a slim chance that the blood test would fail to prove him the father, he was not going to own up to anything. Arrogantly, he said, "Then I'll see you when the baby is born at the blood test lab!" Then he abruptly hung up the phone.

He turned away from the phone on the desk to see one of the office girls looking at him as if he were strange. *Great!* he thought to himself ashamedly, *I wonder how much of that conversation she actually heard. Probably now the whole company will know everything.* But he composed himself enough to walk past her as if nothing happened.

CHAPTER 17

Unhappy Adventure

It was the first nice Sunday in April. Everyone seemed to have spring fever. The seemingly endless bite of winter had finally ended, and the ice disappeared from the streets. The air was slightly damp and promising a little rain. But it was warm and good weather for a light jacket. Danny donned his motorcycle leather late in the morning and headed out for whatever adventures he could find.

His first stop was at Custer's to see what was happening there. *Hm-m! Just a few dummies at the pool table,* he thought. *Let's see if we can interest someone decent in a game so we can get these losers off the table and play some good pool.* So he walked to the side of the bar by the pool tables and set up his shop. He asked Vinnie for a draft beer and then looked around as he light up a cigarette to see who else was in the bar. There were a few old-timers watching the basketball game on the television. Some of those old-timers were pretty good pool players. However, when there was a good game on the TV, they would get so engrossed in the TV that they would never pay very good attention to the pool game.

He was just finishing up his drink while deciding what he wanted to do next when, much to his surprise, Pops bought him a shot of whiskey to go with his beer. After a short while, Danny moved his money and cigarettes around the bar to sit with the old-timers as he returned the favor to Pops. "Vinnie, give Pops a shot of whisky on me."

Time slipped away on Danny. Before he knew it, he drank quite a few beers and shots. He saw another drink coming to him from Jesse. So he stood up and gulped down the last bit of beer in his glass and said, "Jesse, thanks anyway, but if you guys keep buying me drinks, the whole day will be gone, and I will have missed out on all the beautiful weather."

A couple of the old guys looked away from the television long enough to joke with Danny about leaving. Jesse teased, "Oh! What's the matter? Can't even handle a few more drinks?"

Danny chuckled as he waved good-bye and made his hurried exit. As he was putting his helmet on, he noticed the sky was getting darker. He wondered if he should have stayed in the bar for a little while longer for the threat of rain to pass. But it was too late now. He would be embarrassed to go back in. He tried to kick the kick-start to get the engine going, but his foot slipped off the pedal. "Holy cow!" he exclaimed. "I'm not really feeling high. So I'm sure I'm all right to ride. Besides," he reasoned to himself, "I've ridden this bike downright drunk before and never had any problems."

At the first intersection, he pulled to a stop with no problems. So his confidence was renewed, and he continued on. As he rode on a little farther, it started to lightly drizzle. It didn't take long before the streets were all wet. The next intersection had a red light, so he stopped. When the light turned green, he lightly revved the engine as he got the bike into gear, and it started to slide sideways toward the curb. "Oh no!" he exclaimed as the bike went out from underneath him. He managed to step off the bike with his left foot just in time not to get himself hurt. However, the bike landed on its left side and was badly scraped and dented.

"No!" Danny screamed as he picked up the bike. He noticed the shifter was broken off. "Now what am I going to do?" Disgusted, he walked his bike to the closest gas station, which was only a block away. Fortunately for him, the gas station was open. He explained to the attendant what happened and let him know he would be talking to the insurance agency the next day.

He started walking toward home, feeling very upset about leaving his beloved bike at the garage. As he was walking, he realized that if he was going to put in a claim with the insurance agency the next day, he would need a police report. So he made an about-face and headed toward the police station, hoping someone would be there to write up his report. There was a good possibility that there wouldn't be because it was Sunday when most of the police force was off duty.

Luck was with him. There was an officer sitting at the desk behind the glass reading something, maybe a newspaper. He saw Danny and leaned toward the window, "Yes, can I help you?"

"I just had a little accident with my motorcycle, and I need to fill out an accident report to give to the insurance company tomorrow."

Putting down whatever he was reading, the officer looked studiously at Dan and said, "A little accident? Was anyone hurt?"

"No," Danny said thoughtfully as he realized that he had something to be grateful about. "I just damaged the side of my bike. The wheel spun out from under me in the rain."

"Why were you riding a motorcycle in the rain?"

"Well, I didn't expect it to rain until after I got home," Dan sheepishly answered.

"And where were you coming from?" the officer inquired.

Realizing he didn't want to tell the officer he was leaving the bar, he lied and said he was leaving a friend's house.

The officer asked a few other questions like, "Where is the bike now?" and "What exactly happened?" and "How badly was the bike damaged?" Then he made a copy of the report for Danny to take to the insurance company the next day.

After getting his copy of the accident report, Danny headed for home. The walk was pretty long, so he had plenty of time to think about things. And by now, the sky was clear and the sun was shining. *Why couldn't it be like this earlier?* he thought out loud. Then his thoughts turned to Jesse teasing him about not being able to handle another drink. *Man, I wonder what Jesse would say about this.* He felt angry with himself for being so stupid as to ride his bike in the rain. He wondered if his judgment was off because he had too much to drink. A knot in his stomach stayed with him for the whole walk home over his bike being out of commission with the nicer weather arriving.

The following morning, Danny called Veroni Insurance Agency. The voice on the phone sounded familiar as it asked about the location of the bike, but he couldn't quite place it.

"You'll have to come in to fill out some accident forms," the voice said.

"I'll be there in about an hour."

When he entered the claims office door, he was surprised to see Marge smiling at him.

"Marge!" he exclaimed. Then he noticed the brass nameplate sitting on the front of her desk. "Was it you who took my call about an hour ago?" He wasn't quite sure what to expect because in the past Marge didn't seem to be at all fond of him.

"Yes, it was!" she happily replied as she placed the forms on the side of her desk and invited him to sit in the chair next to it. "I filled out as much as I could for you. So now I need you to fill in the diagram and the rest of the information required on the form. When you're done, you will also need to sign it. By the way, do you have an accident report?"

"Yes," Danny replied as he fumbled through his pocket for it and handed it to her.

"Thanks," she said as she took the report. "Do you want a copy for your own records?"

"Yes, please," he humbly replied as he sat down to fill out the form.

Next she asked, "You weren't hurt, were you?"

"No, I was able to get off the bike before it went down."

"Oh, good! I was wondering because it's Monday, and you're not in work," Marge remarked.

"Yeah, well, I'll be going in later," Danny lied. He was thinking of not going in at all that day because he felt so disgusted.

He proceeded to make small talk with Marge so he would at least look like a winner, even if he didn't feel like one. "I knew you left Custer's, but I didn't know you were working here."

"That's right! And I think this is a lot better, don't you?"

"Well, I guess so." Danny could not really see why it was better.

"Of course it is!" Marge's voice almost danced, which caused Dan to look up from his paperwork. "This is a much better job. More class! Better atmosphere! Better lighting even!" she chuckled.

"Yeah! I noticed your name plate!" Danny said with a skeptical look on his face.

Marge chuckled at him, "Seriously, Danny, I loved some of the folks at Custer's, but being around all the booze in a smoky bar and dealing with some of those drunks was making me really depressed. I couldn't take it anymore. And when that guy came in and held the gun to my head ..."

Dan cut in, "Yeah, I heard about that." Now the look on his face seemed to go from skeptical to sort of interested.

Marge continued, "That was it! I started looking around for something better. I really did not want to be in the bar or around all the drinking anymore."

"Yeah, I guess I can't blame you there. But what made you think of insurance?"

Marge chuckled, "Oh, I think my mom might have had something to do with it. She has a friend who is good friends with Mr. Veroni, and she really didn't want me working at the bar and being around all the drinking anymore."

Dan chuckled back and gave an understanding nod. He could see that something changed with Marge and that she didn't seem to hate him anymore. He started to let his guard down.

Giving Dan a very serious look straight in the eye, Marge went on, "Dan, do you know what the coroner wrote on my dad's death certificate? He wrote down that it was a heart attack. But our whole family knows it was the booze that ruined his heart and in the long run brought on the heart attack."

Dan's eyes went back down to the paper he was filling out as he replied, "You really think so?" Worries about his own father began to creep up on him, but he wasn't ready to admit to his concerns.

"Yes, I really think so," Marge sighed.

In denial, Dan remarked with his eyes still down on his paperwork, "My dad drinks as much as your dad ever drank, and he's getting along okay." The expression on Dan's face made it obvious that he didn't like the direction the conversation was going.

Marge thought about how her mother might have answered Dan's remark. "Dan," Marge's voice was stern but soft. She really wanted Dan to consider the seriousness. "That's part of why I'm telling you. Maybe you need to look at your dad's drinking. Maybe he's not doing as well as you think. I hate to say this, but he's drunk almost all the time, and it is very noticeable to everyone who knows him." She paused briefly and looked directly into his eyes. "I'm not trying to make you feel bad, but you may even want to look at your own drinking."

Danny's eyes flashed at Marge as he handed back his completed paperwork, "What? Are you on some high horse now that you're not working in the bar anymore? Don't you worry about him or me. We're both just fine." Dan was done with this conversation.

"Okay, Danny," Marge said in a tone of resignation as she took his paperwork. "See you later."

"Yeah, see you later," Danny sullenly said as he closed the door behind him.

After he got into his car, he quietly thought about what Marge said. And in the meantime, other heavy and disturbing thoughts began to pour into his mind—like demons jabbing at him from all directions. He thought about

Marge's sister, Judy, who was carrying his illegitimate baby and his father who accused him of abandoning the baby. He was angry with himself for spilling his bike and ashamed for getting venereal disease from Hannah. The demons in his head were having a field day throwing at him every accusation they could think of and reminding him of every shameful, guilty, ugly thing going on in his life. He wondered where he was heading in life. Would he turn out like his dad—all depressed and drunk all the time? He felt like such a loser.

He started up his car and gunned the engine. He had a shiny red 1968 Camaro with four in the floor. He loved this car, but now he was feeling very emotional. So he abused it and peeled wheels as he headed down the street. He really did not feel like heading to work in this frame of mind. So he decided to head for home.

When he got in the door, the phone was ringing. It was his father, "You told me you were going to go to the insurance agency this morning on your way to work, but it is eleven o'clock in the morning, and I see that you're at home. Did you take care of things at the insurance agency?"

"Yes, Dad."

"Well, are you coming in to work?" his father said in an angry tone.

"Dad, I hope you can understand. I never take off from work unless there is really a reason. I really don't feel good today. I think I need to stay home."

His father relented from his anger with a loud sigh. "Okay. You'll be going back to work tomorrow, right?"

"Yes, Dad, I will be going back to work tomorrow," Danny replied in a sulky voice. Sometimes it was a disadvantage for Dan to have his father as his boss at work. This was one of those times.

After they hung up, Danny headed for the kitchen. But instead of getting out a beer, he decided to make himself a pot of coffee. He spent the remainder of the day at home trying to put his thoughts together and make sense out of all the messes in his life.

CHAPTER 18

It's a Boy!

It was now early May. Flowers were blooming all around the yard and the ornamental cherry tree on the front lawn of the girls' cottage was a fantasy-like puff of beautiful pink blossoms. It was the Thursday before Mother's Day, and Marge and Judy were having their morning tea and coffee before Marge headed off for work. Judy was due to have her baby any day. The spirits of both girls were animated with anticipation.

"Well, if it's a boy, his name will be Kevin. And if it's a girl, her name will be Valerie," Judy babbled to her sister.

"Hm-m! I like both those names. What will you do if you have twin girls or twin boys?" Marge teased.

Later that day, Marge received a call at work. "Marge, I'm having pains every ten minutes, and the doctor wants me to go in to the hospital."

Marge jumped out of her seat, "I'll be right there."

She didn't even hang up the phone. She just dropped it on her paperwork, grabbed her jacket, and ran out the door after letting Joe and Bob know her sister was having the baby, and she had to go.

She arrived at the cottage eight minutes later to see Judy sitting on the front step with her bag and grinning from ear to ear.

"Okay. Get in!" Marge jumped out of the car and ran around to the other side to open the door for Judy.

Judy laughed at her sister's anxiousness. "Marge, take it easy. We have time. I'm not going to have the baby right this minute, and the hospital is only a few minutes away."

Marge's eyes were both opened wide with worry as she demanded, "You're not going to have the baby in the car on the way there either! You hear me?"

"Don't worry, Marge. It's okay," Judy tried to calm her sister.

The conversation in the car on the way clamored with excitement. "How many minutes apart are the pains now?" Marge asked.

"I don't know. I left my watch at home."

"What!" Marge was horrified.

"The nurse told me to leave all valuables at home. So I figured that for the few minutes it took to get to the hospital, I wouldn't need it. And when we get there, I won't need it anyway. The baby and I will be in the hands of the hospital staff, and we'll be fine."

Marge realized she needed to tone down a notch. So she took a deep breath and breathed out, "I guess." Trying to change the emotional tempo back to the joyful conversation of the morning, Marge asked, "So is it a Kevin or a Valerie?"

Judy paused to think and then said, "It must be a Kevin because this past week, he's been kicking up a storm. I know this. It's a very strong baby."

Marge was calm now. "Judy, I am so excited and happy to be able to be with you for this. It is really wonderful to be able to be here for you to have your baby—my nephew or niece."

When they arrived at the hospital, Judy had to sit in the car for a minute for the labor pain to pass before she could get out. In the meantime, Marge didn't waste a minute. She ran into the hospital to get a nurse and a wheelchair. Before Judy knew what was happening, she was being wheeled into the admittance office. Marge kept complaining about how she couldn't understand why the stupid admittance papers needed to be filled out more than her sister needed to be attended to. "Can't you see she's having a baby!" she kept exclaiming.

The clerk just patiently smiled and finished up with the paperwork. "She'll be fine. She's here at the hospital. She's in good hands. Is this your first experience with someone having a baby, dear?"

Marge was embarrassed. So she forced herself to be calm. In only a few minutes, the nurse was back in to wheel Judy to the labor room.

Once Judy was in the labor room, Marge didn't see her again for about six hours. She found a phone booth and called her mother to let her know Judy was having the baby. Then she went back to the waiting room. The time went by unmercifully slow. "Boy, if there was ever a good time for an excuse to have a good stiff drink, this is it," Marge chided with herself. Then she headed to the coffee shop in the hospital. She wondered what Judy was feeling like at that very moment. She wondered if childbirth was as painful as she heard it was. And the time continued to drag on.

She paid for her coffee and returned to the waiting room to see her mother was sitting there. "Hi, Mom!" She put down her coffee, and they hugged and kissed hello. Marge went on, "They have a coffee shop. Would you like me to get you a cup of coffee?"

"Oh no, Marge. I brought my knitting. That will keep me busy for a while."

Marge chuckled, "So what are you knitting?"

"Well, it's a hat, booties, and a matching blanket for the baby. What do you think?" she asked as she held up the hat and booties.

Marge nodded in approval, "Nice pale green color, Mom! It's not pink or blue. So no matter what, Judy will be able to use it. Good idea."

There was a long silence. Then Marge started to tell her mother how excited she was and about everything that happened up to the time Judy was admitted at the hospital.

Carla Brennan sat quietly and reminisced. "I hope Judy's first baby is as easy as you were to deliver."

"Yeah? What was it like, Mom?"

"Oh boy! I had you real quick. I was in labor a total of three hours. Judy was even quicker. I arrived at the hospital, and an hour and a half later, she was born."

Marge looked at her watch and rolled her eyes up in her head. Judy called her at work around 1:00 p.m. and now it was 4:00 p.m. "Do you think she could be in there until late tonight?"

"Could be! Some women have long labors. I've heard of labors as long as sixteen or eighteen hours. Hopefully, she'll be like me and get it over fast."

"I heard it is really painful. Is it?"

"Oh my! It's been so long I almost forget. Yes, it was quite painful. But once that baby is in your arms, you forget all about the pain. You are just so joyful about that little precious person in your arms."

After a pause, Marge asked, "How did Dad do waiting in the waiting room?"

Carla sighed, "He didn't. When I had you, he gave the nurse the phone number of the bar down the corner and waited there."

"Oh!" Marge's voice dropped as she thought out loud, "I should have known."

"Then he spent all the money he had in his pockets to celebrate. He was so drunk, he didn't even make it in to visit us until the next day, and he was so hung over, the hospital staff almost didn't let him in. He did the same thing again when I had Judy."

Marge looked startled. "Mom, you never told me that before."

"I know. I guess now that he's gone, it doesn't matter anymore. I never told you before because I wanted you to think respectfully of him while he was still alive."

"But now that he's dead, it doesn't matter?" Marge inquired.

"No! No! That's not it!" Carla put her knitting down and looked directly at Marge. "Just think quietly on this for a minute. I'm glad we finally have this opportunity to talk. Just before you moved out on your own, we had a big argument because you thought I should have done more to stop his bad behavior and drinking. By now you know that no one can control another person. The only thing I could do was try to shelter you and your sister from as much of it as I could. I know other women who left their husbands because of their drinking. But every time, it created problems for the kids. It's like you can't win, no matter what you do. Your dad wasn't easy to live with. But he did love you two girls very much. He never cheated on me, and he always brought the money home. Think about it. Where else could I go with two little girls? I couldn't leave you with him. If I went to his parent's home, they also drank. If I went to my parent's home, they were both so sick and old that they would not have fared well with two busy little girls. Now it's over. He's gone, and you are both pretty much grown up. The worst is over, and there is no need to shelter you anymore. We are all free of that stuff now."

Marge sat quietly silent. All the pieces were falling in together. She realized she was looking at her mother through a child's eyes before, and she didn't really understand the full depth of her mother's predicament. She was humbled by her mother's love and sacrifices that she made all those years out of love for her two little girls. Tears welled up in Marge's eyes. She almost spilled her coffee. So she put it down on the end table and got up to walk around.

Carla saw Marge's tears and quickly got up out of her seat to console her. "Marge, please don't feel bad. Someday you'll be a mother. Then you'll understand that mothers sometimes do things that don't always make sense to their kids. I love you so much, honey."

Marge started to blubber a little. "I know, Mom. I know I was very lucky to have a mother like you. I saw a few of the mothers that came into Custer's, and I don't think any of them would make sacrifices like that for their kids. In fact, sometimes they would bring their kids right into the bar with them and drink while their kids played in the bar. They wouldn't even stop their own drinking, let alone put up with all the baloney from their husbands that you did. Mom, I was so wrong. I'm really sorry. I love you too."

If any strangers were to come by at that moment, they might have been seriously taken back by the depth of emotion expressed by the both of them. They cried and hugged with great emotion for quite a few minutes. But what a healing that went on between them! There was a peace and a reconciling between them that only God could understand.

Around six o'clock that evening, the nurse came out to the waiting room. "It's a boy! Eight pounds, ten ounces!"

"Kevin!" Marge exclaimed. "Can we see him?"

Carla put down her knitting. "What a healthy-sized baby!"

The nurse smiled, "You can see him in the nursery window in a short while. We are still cleaning him up. But if you want to see Judy, you can both go see her in the recovery room. In fact, she asked to see you both." Within only a few minutes they were all in the recovery room, bubbling with excitement over the new wonder that came into the world.

CHAPTER 19

The Accident

The Saturday morning following Kevin's birth, Ed Schisler was at Custer's bar tying on a drunk. Arnie Sayer, one of the old-timers, sat down with Pops, Jesse, and Ed and ordered a round of shots for the whole group. "Ed," he said and respectfully nodded to Ed as the group of men drank down their shots together.

Ed looked puzzled and knitted his eyebrows together. He knew that nod was special, but he didn't know why Arnie nodded at him like that. Arnie saw Ed's look of confusion and said, "You know that Judy had the baby, right? You know you're a grandfather now, right?"

"What?" Joyful surprise filled Ed's face. "How did you find out? Tell me more."

"Connie, my daughter, who is a nurse at the hospital, said he was born Thursday night around 6:00 p.m."

"He?"

"Yeah! A boy, eight pounds, ten ounces. She named him Kevin."

With that bit of news, Ed joyfully ordered a round of shots. "Give us all the good stuff, Vinnie. Whatever they want!" As the drinks were on the way, Ed was quietly thinking to himself about what he should do next. *Danny doesn't care. So it's silly to dash home to tell him. Boy, I'd love to see that baby. Maybe if I go to the hospital I can see the baby.*

As they finished their shots, Ed got up from his stool, "Thanks for telling me, Arnie." He collected his money off the bar, left his tip for Vinnie, and then he told the old-timers he was going to see the baby as he headed out the door and down the street toward the hospital. He was so oblivious between the drinks and his excitement that he did not see the traffic light turn green where he was crossing the street. The approaching driver did not expect Ed to step off the curb and hit him with the right front fender of his car.

Mayhem took over. People standing by screamed. Traffic stopped. A few nearby men surrounded him to keep people away from him and to wave off oncoming traffic while someone went to call the ambulance. Within minutes, the corner was swarming with emergency responders and policemen.

Danny's friend, Fred Dietz, was in a store across the street buying cigarettes when the whole thing happened. "What the …!" he exclaimed in disbelief. He was completely shocked by what he saw. His hands shook as he quickly gave the cashier the money to pay for his cigarettes and dashed out the door.

"Oh wow! I can't believe it." Fred was totally dazed when he realized that it really was Mr. Schisler that he saw get hit by the car and who was now lying unconscious by the curb in a large pool of blood with his trousers and shirt heavily soaked by the blood he lay in.

"Is he breathing?" Fred asked one of the emergency responders.

"He's breathing, but he doesn't look very good at all. You need to get out of the way. Please move away from the area, son."

"Yeah, but he's my friend's dad," Fred cried out.

"He is? Can you tell me his name and how to get a hold of his family?"

Fred gave the man all the information and then told him he would get his only surviving son and meet them at the hospital emergency room.

Fred took one last look at him. "Wow! I can't believe it."

Pops saw Fred running toward his car and stopped him. "Where are you going?" he asked.

"I'm going to get Danny," Fred stated frantically.

"Be very careful what you say to Danny. His father got hit while he was heading to the hospital to see Danny's baby. I think Danny would be devastated if he knew that," Pops warned.

"Oh, wow! That's awful! Oh, God, please help!" Fred shouted as he ran to his car. The sight of Ed lying in his blood in the street filled his head the whole way there. In only a few minutes, he was at Danny's front door. He knocked furiously and screamed for Danny. Danny only hollered out the window from his bed, "Go away, man, I'm sleeping. It's ten o'clock in the morning. Can't I sleep in one morning of the week?"

Fred didn't wait any more. He opened the front door and let himself in. He ran up the stairs to Danny's room going two steps at a time. "Danny, Danny, you got to get up!" he screamed as he shook him in his bed.

"Are you crazy? What is your problem, coming into the house like this and waking me up?"

"It's your dad. He's been hit by a car. He's been in a bad accident. Get up!"

"Huh?" Danny jumped out of bed and saw the frenzy in Fred's eyes. "Are you serious?"

"Of course I'm serious!"

Suddenly Danny realized by the way Fred was behaving that what he said happened, really happened.

Fred threw Danny's jeans at him. "You think I would be doing all this for a joke?"

As Danny hurriedly put his jeans on, Fred found a shirt and threw that at him also. Danny dressed so fast, he could feel his hands shake. "Is he really bad?"

"He was out cold, and I saw blood."

"A lot?" Danny was probing for information.

Fred could see they both needed to collect themselves. So he lied, "No, just a little." The sight of Ed lying in his blood with his clothing all soaked flashed into his mind again. He tried to tell himself that it may not be all that serious after they clean him up and bring him to consciousness.

The both of them got into Danny's Camaro and sped away to the hospital. On the way, Fred filled Danny in on what he knew about the incident so far and about what he heard from other people who were at the scene. Without thinking, he told Danny that his father was heading to the hospital when he got hit. Then he realized that now he would have to tell Danny why his dad was heading there.

"What was he going to the hospital for?" Danny asked.

Fred turned his head to look out the window as he mumbled, "He heard Judy had her baby, and he wanted to go see it." He could see from the corner of his eye Danny's shoulders drop forward as if someone hit him in the heart. They were quiet for the rest of the ride there.

When they arrived at the emergency room, it was filled with clamor. There were a lot of people waiting in the waiting room and a lot of nurses and medical attendants running around. When Danny and Fred told the woman at the admitting desk they were there to see Ed Schisler, she called a nurse in the hallway. The nurse came over and gave them her most reassuring smile and then instructed them to have a seat in the waiting room for a few minutes. But before they could even find a seat, she called out to them, "The doctor said you could go in to see him." Her expression was much different now. It looked very concerned. Danny gulped. Somehow, he knew that was not a good sign.

Danny went in to see his father with his friend, Fred, behind him. Another nurse was standing next to Ed's bed reading his life support systems. Ed was in a hospital gown with a sheet pulled up to his chest. He was still out cold.

"Dad?" Danny called to him. But there was no response.

"I'm afraid he doesn't hear you right now, son," the nurse said to him.

Danny could feel tears welling up in his eyes. "Is he going to live?"

The nurse paused, trying to figure out the best way to answer him. "It doesn't look good."

Danny somehow knew this meant the worst. One tear rolled down onto Danny's cheek. Then he could hold back no more and sobbed his heart out. Fred felt Dan's pain with him. He put his arm around him as the tears poured from his eyes, too. Then the two young men sat calmly next to the bed waiting for Ed to expire. They talked about his dad, the past, and what Danny would do with his life now. A fear began to settle over Dan as he remembered the intense loneliness and depression his father used to suffer with all the time. Dan wondered what he would do if, or when, his father passed away. Thoughts of the baton of depression and loneliness being passed from his father to him filled him with intense anxiety. And in spite of the fact that they both knew Ed died while heading to the hospital to see Judy and the baby, all talk about them was firmly avoided.

A short while later, the life support systems went quiet and the nurse started unhooking the wires from Ed's body. She softly announced to Dan and Fred that he died. The room was strangely peaceful and quiet. Danny went over to his father and then tearfully looked at Fred, who took this as his cue to look away as Danny kissed his father good-bye. Then the two young men silently left the room.

As they walked through the waiting room, they saw Pops and Jesse, who both jumped out of their seats as soon as they saw them. "How is he?" Pops asked.

"He's dead," Danny mumbled.

"Oh no! Really?" Jesse said.

Pop's cut in, "We saw him this morning at Custer's. It all happened so fast."

Jesse started up again, "He was heading to the hospital, so excited to see the baby. Then it happened. Just that fast …" Jesse paused. Pops gave Jesse a wide-eyed stare, signaling to him to shut his mouth.

It was too late. Danny darted out of the hospital with Fred. Pops and Jesse charged out after him. They managed to stop him by the car. "Whoa, pal!" Pops hollered to him. "Wait! Please!" When they caught up to him, Pops continued. "Danny, me and some of your dad's friends have been talking. I know you and Ed did not really have any family around, and you could probably use some help with arranging the funeral and burial, right?"

Dan looked at Fred because that is one of the things they discussed while they were waiting for Ed to expire. "Well, I thought I would just have to call the funeral parlor and make the arrangements," Danny said as he lowered his head.

"Me and some of your dad's other friends would like to help you with this. Would you let us help you?"

"Sure." Danny displayed no emotion, but inside he was grateful for the support. Just losing his father was more than he was prepared to handle for one day, let alone try to figure out what to do for the funeral and burial arrangements.

"Me and Jesse will meet you at your home in about fifteen minutes, okay?"

"Okay," red-eyed Danny conceded.

Danny and Fred went in Danny's car, and Pops and Jesse went in Jesse's car. On the way, Pops and Jesse talked.

"You know, Jesse, before the baby was born, Ed was telling us that Danny didn't want anything to do with that baby. Don't you remember that?"

"I really wasn't thinking, Pops. It just blurted out of my mouth."

Pops continued on, "Now I'm wondering if that boy thinks he's somehow responsible for his father's death. I mean, just think about it! He knows his father was heading to the hospital to see Judy's baby—his illegitimate son. I'll bet he feels somehow that he's guilty for his father dying like that."

Jesse remorsefully added, "I thought about that after I opened my stupid mouth. Sometimes I hate myself."

"Oh stop, Jesse. We all make mistakes. I just wish there was something we could do to help him get through this."

Jesse shook his head in amazement as he contemplated. "Ed was really overjoyed about that baby! I couldn't believe how much that baby meant to him."

Rubbing his chin, Pops responded, "He sure was. I've got to have a talk with Danny about that baby. It would break Ed's heart if Danny abandoned that baby, especially after he grew up as an orphan and felt so abandoned himself."

"Oh boy! Be careful," Jesse warned. "You could be stepping into a really bad scene if you're not careful."

After a few seconds of silence, Pop continued, "It might not be as difficult as you think to persuade him. Who else does Danny have? You know how Ed would go on about being alone in the world and how he was raised an orphan because his parents abandoned him. Danny must have heard that a million times. It's got to be on his mind that he could go through life with those same ugly, lonely feelings. You know what? I've got to do this for me, so I can feel better about all this. Not for Danny. I just can't stand to see this go on for another generation."

"You're going to do it for yourself?" Jesse couldn't understand how Pops would be doing it for himself.

"Yes, for me—and for this baby. I can't let a terrible legacy like that continue. No child should go through life feeling abandoned by his father like that."

"I never really thought about it that way, Pops." Then Jesse chuckled, "You've got to forgive me for laughing, but I was just remembering how melodramatic Ed would get. He was so pathetic sometimes. I hope you can get through to that kid. You're right. It would be very sad to see a legacy like that continue. I think it would not only hurt Danny's child, but eventually it would come back to hurt Danny too. Don't you agree?"

"Yes, I do." Pops rubbed his face, deep in thought. "I've got to really give some thought to how I will go about getting through to Danny."

CHAPTER 20

The funeral was brief and simple. The viewing was Tuesday, and Ed was buried on Wednesday. As it turns out, Danny was able to find a piece of paper in one of Ed's drawers with contact information for his mother's relatives in England. When they called the numbers, they were able to contact his grandmother and aunt, and they did fly in from England to come to the funeral. A few coworkers from Ed's and Danny's work place and a few friends from around town also attended. And a couple of Danny's closest friends whom he knew since his childhood, including Fred, stayed with him at his home until the funeral was over so he wouldn't be alone through it all.

Apparently his grandmother and aunt had money, so they could afford to stay at a nearby hotel until the viewing and funeral were all over. They also helped Danny with some of the funeral expenses.

When he met his relatives for the first time, it was rather awkward because he really didn't know them. In fact, he was relieved that he could even recognize them, which was only possible because of the pictures on his father's dresser. Strangely enough, the pictures were on the dresser before Beth, his mother, died. And Dan's father never removed them. The pictures just stayed on the dresser all these years, like a melancholic memory. Of course his aunt and grandmother were about twenty years older than they were in the pictures, but they still looked much the same. As they entered the door at the funeral home, Danny cordially greeted them and made sure they were accommodated throughout the couple of days they were in town.

Wednesday morning, before the burial, his grandmother and aunt tried to persuade him to come to England to live with them. They expressed concern about Beth's son, being alone in the world. Pops overheard them talking and moved to stand closer so he could hear everything being said. Danny seemed unsure of what he wanted to do. He didn't want to be alone in the world. The fear of that pain was becoming too real for him—especially now that his only real family member was gone. However, he didn't really feel comfortable about going to England with them either. After all, they were basically strangers to him because he never even met them before.

After the burial service, the funeral party went to Danny's home for a final gathering. Pops and all the rest of the old-timers chipped in and paid for light sandwiches and beverages to be served to the guests. People all sat around, chatted, and gave Danny their condolences.

In the meantime, Pops was looking for a moment when he could get Danny alone. The guests were starting to trickle out the door, and Danny headed up the stairs for the bathroom. Pops saw his opportunity and quietly followed up behind him. The moment Pops saw him come out, he asked Danny if he had a minute to talk.

"Uh, sure." Then Dan motioned Pops to follow him to his bedroom.

As they entered the room, Pops started the discussion, "You understand, Danny, I'm very concerned about you because you were my friend's son."

Danny looked Pops in the eyes, and then turned his face down to the floor and shook his head. "Pops, I have to tell you how much I really appreciate what you, and Jesse, and the others have done in helping me with this funeral and all the arrangements. Besides feeling so bad, I really had no idea what to do next. This whole thing has just been so unreal."

Then Danny sat down on the bed, and Pops sat down next to him. "Think nothing of it, son. We were all so happy to be able to do something to help. We were all really concerned for you, and we all know it's been difficult for you. We're sort of like family because we've known you since you were just a little boy."

"Yeah," Danny sighed.

"Have you thought about what you will be doing with your life now that your dad is gone?"

"Not really. My grandmother and aunt were trying to talk me into moving to England with them."

Pops softly inquired, "Is that something you would really want to do?"

Danny buried his hands in his thick dark locks as if it would help him collect his thoughts. "Well, they seem nice enough. But it's not just a matter of getting on a plane and going. I have my home here, my job, and my friends. I know this town. It's home to me." Danny sat up straight and continued, "And I don't really know my relatives from England. I'd be giving up everything I have here to go to a place where I don't know anyone or anything."

Pops smiled as though in relief. "You're very fortunate in one thing. Even though you lost your father, and I'm sure you're going to miss him, he left you good. Not every man owns a home outright at twenty years old."

"Yeah, I guess you're right." Danny smiled faintly, but his following sigh showed that his smile was not sincere.

Pops continued, "You don't have to be alone you know."

"Yeah?" Danny looked curiously at Pops and wondered what was coming next.

Pops very cautiously considered how to start this conversation. "Danny, you know everything could be worse. You've had a good life, and your father took good care of you. You at least had the blessing of knowing your father and knowing that he loved you all your life. What if it was all different? What if your father was alive, but he didn't want you or care about you? What if he put you in an orphanage and abandoned you?"

Pops' words hit Danny hard. Guilt immediately pierced him. Without Pops actually coming right out and saying it, he knew Pops was talking about what he was doing to his own child. He really didn't expect Pops to say anything that would hurt so badly. His poor choices about Judy and the baby filled his heart with remorse. He felt ashamed to consider that his own child might suffer from the same pain of abandonment that father did. He sat quietly and stared at the floor, wondering what he should do.

Pops didn't know exactly what was going on in Danny's head, but he could see that he was getting somewhere so he continued. "You can't keep going on the way I see you going. All the girls and the partying get old fast, and you'll find it's not what it's cracked up to be. Right now, it may seem like fun. But as the years wear on, and you find yourself in trouble a few times, you'll wish you did things differently. Believe me! You'll probably even start to hate all that stuff."

There was a long silence. Pops decided to let Danny think for a minute or two.

No longer did the empty flings with a multitude of pretty girls seem so appealing. Certainly the experience of picking up a disease from Hannah was not a happy memory. He knew what Pops said was right because he had begun to actually feel hate for Hannah. Drinking didn't look like a very promising pursuit either as he remembered his conversation with Marge about her father's drinking being the cause of his death, and now his own father was dead at least in part because of his drinking. He even felt angry with himself for the damage his did to his bike after drinking shots with the old-timers at Custer's. Then his thoughts turned to life ahead. He dreaded the idea of spending his life alone. The reality finally crashed over him that all the drinking, partying, and girls in the world would never fill the empty hole of loneliness that was ahead of him.

Pops paused to consider how to make the next statement. "Even for yourself, it's not good to live your life all alone. But you don't have to be alone and neither does your baby. You know, Danny, I'm an old man now. I'm retired. My wife's dead. It's just me at home. Sometimes it's nice because I'm free to come and go as I please, but it does get lonely. But I'm very lucky. I still have my kids. I have a family, and even though they're not around all the time, I'm never lonely for the holidays, and they do come to see me sometimes. Whenever my kids and their families get together, they make sure I'm there with them. And I look forward to it. If I feel lonely, I can always call them. They're always there for me. A family is a great thing to have." Pops paused again. "Besides that, a real man would take responsibility for his baby, for his family."

It never occurred to Danny before that it might be a manly thing to care for one's wife and children. He remembered how depressing Christmas could be with his father because his mother was gone. But at least his father was there for him. If his father wasn't there all his years of growing up, he would have been in the same lonely, miserable state that his orphaned father had been in all his life. He thought about what future Christmases might be like without his father being around. He felt anxious thinking about what it would be like to live alone in that house. His fear of loneliness suddenly became oppressive. He became increasingly aware that when the funeral party was over, and his friends who had been staying around to comfort him went home, he would be totally alone. Suddenly the idea of having a wife and a child to share his home and his life was very appealing.

"Pops, do you think I should marry Judy?" he blurted out with an embarrassed look on his face.

Pops sat erect with surprise at Danny's directness. He cautiously proceeded, "Well, yeah! That might be a good thing. After all, she has your baby. And you have to admit, Judy is a really beautiful, sweet girl."

Danny held his face in his hands. He was really struggling with his feelings. "Pops, you're right. She really is a sweet, beautiful girl. I didn't really appreciate her like I should have, but I surely do now. How stupid I was! I wish I didn't treat her like such a jerk." Then Danny turned and looked Pops in the eyes. "The last time I saw her, I left her bawling her eyes out because I told her I didn't want anything to do with the baby, and I wasn't about to marry her. She probably hates me and doesn't want anything to do with me. And what was the matter with me anyway? You would think I would have cared about Judy and that baby after all the years of listening to my father moaning about being orphaned and how much more lonely he got because of losing my mother."

Pops continued trying to persuade Danny. "I wouldn't worry about Judy being mad at you. In fact, I think maybe you should go see her and the baby. I know for fact that they're home now because Arnie's daughter is a nurse at the hospital, and she said Judy and Kevin left the hospital to go home. Maybe …"

Danny cut him off. "Kevin?"

"Yeah! That's the baby's name. Didn't you know that?"

"No!" Danny looked at Pops incredulously, "A boy?"

"Yeah!" Pops was mystified. "I guess with everything going on, no one told you the details."

Danny stood up and anxiously looked around. "Yeah, I knew the baby was born. I just didn't know what kind. A boy! Wow!"

"What kind? Does it make a difference if it is a boy or a girl?" Pops questioned.

"I know it sounds stupid after all my terrible behavior, but I was really hoping for a son," Danny said as he combed his hair in the mirror. "Do you think it would be weird for me to go see Judy and the baby after everybody leaves today, so soon after the funeral?"

"No! Certainly not," Pops replied, trying to compose himself. "What are you going to say to her?"

Danny stopped and looked directly at Pops. "I'm not sure yet. I don't really know if Judy would even let me in the door. But I'd like to see my son. Wow! I really regret the way I treated her that day in the cornfield when she told me. I hope she won't be mad at me." Then he rolled his eyes up to the ceiling with a desperate look on his face. "I really was so mean to her the last time I saw her. I feel so bad about it. What do you think? Do you think she'll let me in to see her and the baby?"

"M-m-m!" Pops thoughtfully answered, "You won't know until you try. You've got to give it a try to find out. Even if she kicks you out, I think it would be the right thing to do, son."

"Well, I'm certainly going to give it a try," Danny responded as he pulled his face, thinking of what to say and how he was going to approach Judy.

"Listen," Pops said. "If it doesn't work out, don't give up. Try again later. Women like to say *no*, but they can only say it so many times. In fact I think they like it when you're persistent and keep trying after they say *no* to you. The persistence makes them feel loved."

"Uh-h, okay," Dan said with a befuddled look on his face.

Both men stood up from the bed and gave each other a warm hug. The hug was brief however because Dan was anxious to go downstairs and get the funeral over with.

CHAPTER 21

The Visit

As soon as most of the people from the funeral gathering left, Danny started to clean up. Some people were still lingering, but Danny didn't care. He was anxious. Pops saw what he was doing and called Jesse, Arnie, and Fred to help with the cleanup. When the remaining people saw the cleaning going on, they politely left also. Danny's aunt and grandmother came over to him to say their good-byes.

"Let us know what you plan to do," his aunt said as she hugged him good-bye.

"I hope you don't mind, but I think I'm going to stay here since this is where my job, my home, and all my friends are," Danny said softly. He then turned to his grandmother so he could hug her good-bye. They both told Danny to be sure to keep in touch.

"I surely will," Danny politely replied.

Soon all the cleanup was done, and Pops and the other old-timers were all heading out the door. Danny indicated to Fred that it was time for everyone else to leave also.

Fred was expecting to stay with Danny a little while after the funeral party left. So he was surprised to see Danny wanted to leave. "You're leaving too, Dan?"

"Yeah! You're not going to believe this, but I'm going to see Judy and the baby," Danny replied. As they headed out the door, he then proceeded to tell Fred all about his conversation with his relatives about going to England and then about his conversation with Pops and his decision to go see Judy and the baby.

"Wow! Good luck," Fred wished him. "I wouldn't want to have to do that. You got more brass than I thought."

Dan chuckled. "It's time for me to be responsible. I think this is what Dad would want me to do, and I don't want to do to my son what my father's parents did to him. It's time for me to be a man, the kind of man that takes care of his family and doesn't waste his life getting into trouble. The conversation I had with Pops was exactly what I needed to hear. I really feel bad about what a jerk I've been. And I can't believe that I was throwing away my own son." Dan stopped to look Fred in the eye. "You know what, Fred? I really enjoyed hearing Pops tell me how much he enjoys having his family around him. It made me realize that I want that same thing. I want to have a family. Besides all that, I've got a responsibility to this little boy. He's my son. I'm responsible for his life. And I've got a responsibility to his mother." The expression in Danny's face was dead serious.

"Oh, wow!" Fred teased. "Whatever happened to you? I hope it don't catch on. I've still got some partying to do."

Danny realized how intense his mood was, and they both laughed.

Then Danny continued, "Oh yeah! Well, now I'm really going to blow your mind. I'm planning to ask Judy to marry me—maybe even today."

"Holy cow!" Fred looked shocked. "You are really full of surprises! Judy is still kind of young and a little flaky. Are you sure you want to do this?"

Danny shot an angry look at Fred. "I'm going to try. And if she is old enough to have my baby, she is old enough for me to marry."

Fred realized he hit a nerve with Dan and was quick to change the subject. "So, how do you like the name *Kevin?*"

Danny's reply was sullen. "It's a good name. It's manly. It's too late if I don't like it anyway. She already named him. That's the name on his birth certificate. I'm just sorry I wasn't there for him to be born. And I regret that I already missed out on his first week of life. But that's all about to change." He tightened his lips as he headed to his car, determined to make good from this point forward.

"Good luck, Dan. I'll be cheering for you," Fred said as they parted.

Danny smiled back at his friend and said, "Thanks." Then he got into the Camaro and drove off. As he drove along, anxiety began to set in. He asked himself a million questions, like *What will she think when she sees me pull up in front of the house? Is she going to be mad at me? Will she ever forgive me? Will she even let me in? Who's going to be there with her? What will they think of me?*

How will they treat me? What if she breaks down and cries? Danny's mind was going like a whirlwind. His hand shook as he grabbed the shifter to change gears. "Oh man!" he said out loud to himself. "Look at me. I can't believe it. I'm shaking!"

Making a concerted effort, Danny was able to pull himself back together. "Whatever will be, will be." Then he laughed as he remembered what Pops said about how women can only say *no* so many times, and persistence makes them feel loved. It was funny because Pops' words actually gave him encouragement regardless how ludicrous they sounded.

When he pulled up in front of Marge's cottage, it was early evening, and there were two other cars parked there. So he had to park across the street. *Oh man!* he thought to himself. *There's other people there. I wonder who it is. This could be really awkward!* As he shut his car door, he wondered if this event would be embarrassing or not.

Before he could knock on the front door, Marge opened it. "Come in," she warmly welcomed. Danny sheepishly looked around to see who was there as he walked in. It was Carla Brennan and Bill Bach. Danny cleared his throat. "Hi! Where's Judy?"

"Oh, did you come to see the baby?" Carla asked as obligingly as she could.

"Yeah, and Judy too," Danny answered a little nervously. "They are both here, right?"

"Oh yes, dear! Let me go see if Judy is decent. She was just napping with the baby."

Carla went into Judy's room to tell her Danny was here. Then Dan heard Judy exclaim out loud, "Danny? Wait a minute. I want to put on something presentable."

Then he heard Carla quietly say to Judy, "Yes, that's a good idea. By the way, I think that maybe Danny would like to see you and the baby alone."

"Okay, Mom," Judy replied. "I'll let you know when we're ready for him to come in. Just give me a minute."

Her mother then came out to tell Danny that Judy would be just a minute. "Would you like a cup of coffee while you're waiting? It's real perked coffee, not Marge's instant!"

Danny calmed down considerably. He realized that they were all being very hospitable to him, regardless of what they might have thought of him. "Yes, coffee would be very good. Thank you."

Marge poured Danny a cup of coffee and very shortly after Judy came out and invited Danny in to see the baby. As they went in, Judy shut the door behind them, and Carla folded her hands in prayer. Bill gave her an understanding look, and then leaned forward in his seat and bowed his head as if to be joining her with his own prayers.

As soon as Danny got into the room, he headed straight for the bassinet. There he saw a sleeping little bundle with one hand sticking out from under his blanket. Danny touched his hand, "Kevin! Wow! Look at him! He's incredible!"

Judy had a questioning look on her face as she asked, "Do you like the name?"

"Sure! It's a great name. I like it. How are you both doing anyway?"

"Real good." Judy paused proceeded cautiously. "I'm surprised to see you," she said as she sat on the bed. "Wasn't the funeral and burial today?"

"Yeah," Danny replied with ambivalence. "I guess you would be surprised."

Judy didn't know what to expect. So she silently sat down on the bed and waited for him to go on.

"I'm really going to miss my father," he softly went on. "Sometimes you don't know how much you love someone until they're gone."

Judy understood all too well from her own experience with her father's passing. "I'm really sorry about your dad, Danny."

Danny just stared at the baby. He couldn't believe the baby was really his own flesh and blood. "Wow! He's really neat!" Danny exclaimed.

"Yeah," Judy passively agreed as she waited for Danny to go on.

"Judy, I've been thinking about things. I've been a real jerk. I hope you'll forgive me. This is my baby too. I can't give up on him, and I'm very sorry for the way I treated you. If you're mad at me, I don't blame you."

Judy calmly replied, "Well, I was mad at you and very hurt. But I think I've been even madder at myself for being such a stupid kid to think you'd want to marry me just because I was having your baby."

Danny turned away from the baby and sat down next to her with a big sigh. "You're not a stupid kid." He composed himself for what he wanted to say next. "You're a sweet, wonderful person, and I'm sure you're a good mother." He took a deep breath and then blurted out, "I was just hoping you wouldn't mind being my wife, too."

Judy caught her breath. She wanted to throw her arms around him, but she resisted. She didn't want to do anything impulsive. She had too much responsibility at risk. She looked at him. Then she calmly looked down at the floor.

"Since Dad died, the house is mine. You and Kevin could move in with me at my house."

"You don't have to bribe me, Danny." Tears streamed over Judy's thick lashes onto her cheeks. "I've always wanted to marry you, but if it means I have to deal with the drinking, the bars, and the partying, it's not happening. All that stuff has to go. We've both seen it mess up too many people in our lives. I'm taking a firm stand on this. And I mean it! This is my last stand! I just won't accept any of that baloney. That's it."

Danny saw she meant business and humbly lowered his chin. "I don't want the drinking, the bars, or the partying anymore either. My father was in the bar drinking just before he got hit by that car."

Then Judy remembered what Marge told her about Danny and Hannah. "I will not accept you seeing any other girls either. I will not accept any of that free-love hippie stuff."

Dan gulped his guilt down. He realized that Marge must have told Judy about the episode that night at Custer's. "Oh Judy, I don't know what you might have heard. Maybe Marge told you some things about me. I've done some stupid stuff, and messing around with girls is really wrong. I regret what I've done. In fact, what you and I did was wrong. But I'm hoping to make things right. I hope you'll forgive me. And of course, you would be the only one! And I'm not into that hippie free-love stuff either." He reached for both of her hands and looked imploringly into her eyes. "I really don't want anyone else but you." He paused a few seconds, "And our baby."

Judy decided to make one more demand. "And if we get married and become a family, I would like for us all go to church on Sunday too. I want my son, I mean *our* son, to grow up right, knowing morals, values, and standards, so he doesn't make a mess of his life like some of the rest of us have."

Danny was taken aback by the church requirement. "Do you go to church?"

"No," she said defensively. "But I'm going to start as soon as I can take Kevin out places with me. And that's whether we get married or not! Mom suggested it. And I thought it sounded like a good idea. I really want to start living right. I really want Kevin to grow up right."

Danny pensively answered, "Judy, sweetie, whatever you say sounds good to me."

"Really?" Judy asked almost unbelievingly.

Dan looked her in the face and softly said, "Really!"

"Then yes, I'll marry you," Judy joyfully answered.

Danny gave a big sigh of relief as he pulled her toward him to hug her. He held her for a long time, partly because he was so happy, and partly because he didn't want her to see the tears welled up in his eyes. But she pulled away to look adoringly at him and saw them.

"You know what, Danny?" Judy giggled, "I really like when you call me *sweetie*." She started to get up. "In fact, this is the happiest day of my life. We've got to go tell everyone."

He pulled her back to her seat as he chuckled. "Please, let's not go out and tell everyone until our eyes dry up."

So they sat and talked for a while longer, amusing themselves with how great it would be to watch Kevin grow up and the years ahead. Life was so full of promise. Their hearts were so full of joy. Then their conversation turned to making their plans for their wedding day.

First Danny presented his idea to Judy. "We could have a justice of the peace come to our home to marry us with our friends and family to watch. Then afterward, have a party either in the house or on the lawn. What do you think?"

"That sounds nice," Judy responded. "But I'd like to have it at the church. Maybe Mom's pastor would marry us, and then we could go to the basement for a small party. I've actually been dreaming about this long before you ever came to propose. I know it sounds silly because I really had no idea if it would ever happen or not. But I've already given this considerable thought."

Danny looked at her in speechless amazement, as Judy continued. "I'd really like to have a party at the church because then we would have less trouble convincing people that they can't drink at our wedding party."

Danny straightened up as his eyebrows went up. "Wow! Are you serious?"

"Yes, I am," Judy replied in a firm voice.

"Sure, sweetie," Danny said as he looked down at the floor and wondered what it would be like to go to a wedding without any drinking. "Do you think any of our guests will be offended?"

"Danny, if they're offended, they don't have to come. I am just not having it. You do understand, don't you?" Judy looked look at Danny with a slightly worried look on her face.

"Judy, sweetie, if that is what you want, I'm going to stand with you on it. No drinking at our wedding party! I just have one question. What if the church isn't available? I've heard of that happening before."

Judy thought about it for a second or two. "Well, we'll see what days are available and make the best we can of it. If worse comes to worse, we can have it at your house, I mean our home. But it will still be a booze-free party, or it isn't happening, Danny. I really mean it."

Danny was taken aback by how strong Judy was about having no booze at the wedding. "Judy, I really do love you. And I'm really proud of you for taking such a strong stand on this. Whatever you want, I will go along with it. In fact, I really like your idea. No booze!"

Judy was so thrilled. She wrapped her arms around Danny. "I love you too! I am so happy!" After they hugged for a few seconds, Judy pulled away and asked, "Oh! One more thing! Will you be giving me an engagement ring?"

Danny was a little embarrassed. "Wow! I guess I'm a typical guy. I didn't even think of it. But yes! I will get you a really nice engagement ring and a beautiful wedding band to match. And you'll have your engagement ring by this weekend. I promise! Are you going to add anymore contingencies to our wedding agreement?"

Judy giggled with embarrassment. "No. But let's go tell the others while Kevin is still quiet."

So the two of them quietly went out and shut the door behind them to tell Judy's mother, Marge, and Bill the good news. They found Carla and Bill sitting on the sofa watching the television, and Marge was sitting on the floor next to her mother.

"Mom, we want to tell you something," Judy coyly announced.

"Yes dear!" Both of Carla's eyebrows were raised with pleasant hope.

"We're going to get married."

With that, Carla, Marge, and Bill all jumped out of their seats to hug and congratulate the couple. It was a joyous clamor that went on among them as they all jumped around and hugged each other. After that, they all sat down and drank coffee as Judy and Danny discussed their ideas for the wedding plans. It was a warm and wonderful time of family bonding as they all shared in working out the wedding plans.

CHAPTER 22

The Wedding Day

It was early Saturday morning on a beautiful late June day. All the trees were in full green foliage. It was warm, and the birds were singing joyously throughout the neighborhood, as if they were joining in on the celebration. The wedding was rather small. Only a little over thirty people attended. And it was held at the church where Judy's mother and her mother's friend, Bill Bach, attended worship service every Sunday. During the wedding ceremony, Carla held her six-week-old grandson while he chirped and cooed just as happily as the birds outside the church.

When the wedding ceremony was over, the picture taking began. Judy looked beautiful in her white lace midi-length wedding gown. Her huge brown eyes with the long, thick eyelashes fluttered as she and Danny posed for their wedding pictures in front of the church. The granite steps and the large carved wooden doors on the front of the church made a beautiful background for the pictures to be taken.

Judy and Danny decided to save money by having all their friends and family take all the wedding pictures for them rather than hire a professional photographer. So there was a flurry of chaotic activity going on while all the pictures were being taken. In the meantime, Carla was waiting patiently in front of the church rocking the baby carriage. And while she was waiting, it seemed everyone wanted to see the baby. They all got a real kick out of Kevin because each time someone came close, he flailed his little arms and legs with excitement.

When everyone was finally done taking their pictures, all the people headed through the side door of the church to the basement where the food and refreshments were waiting. Once they were all down there, Kevin fell asleep in his little carriage, probably tired from all the previous excitement. While he slept, Judy and Danny went around to all the guests to say *hello* and *thank you for coming*. The ladies were all quite impressed with her beautiful half-carat engagement ring. And Pops, Jesse, and Arnie were happily sitting together with platefuls of food and soda pop.

The best man for the wedding ceremony was Fred, and the maid of honor was Marge. As best man, Fred had the honors of doing their wedding toast just before they left for their honeymoon. "Hey! I can't believe I'm doing a wedding toast with ginger ale," he exclaimed incredulously. "Since when do you drink ginger ale for a wedding toast?"

Judy and Danny both gave him big smiles, and the crowd laughed politely.

He continued, "Anyway, to a wonderful couple! May God bless you both! And I guess since I just lost my best pool partner, I'll have to find someone and get married too."

With that, everyone laughed heartily and cheered for the couple as they drank their ginger ale toast.

After the party was over, Judy and Danny had plans to go to the seashore for the weekend for their honeymoon. Not only did Danny's bosses at the print shop make him the foreman since his father's passing, but they also gave him Monday and Tuesday off with pay so he could have a long weekend with his new wife. As the couple got into the Camaro with a *Just Married!* message painted with white shoe polish on the back windshield and tin cans tied to the back bumper, everyone cheered and wished them well as they drove off.

After all the guests left, Marge, Carla, and Bill stayed behind to finish cleaning up the church while Kevin slept in his baby carriage. Carla agreed to take care of her grandson while Judy and Danny were away.

As Marge was energetically gathering up all the paper table covers and paper plates, she said to her mother, "Well, it looks like a great weekend to be at the shore. But the weather reports are saying the water is not supposed to be so warm for swimming." Then she quickly added, "But it will certainly be beautiful weather for walking on the beach and going on a boat ride."

Carla replied, "Yes, God has blessed them with some beautiful weather."

"Mom," Marge carefully considered how she was going to say what was on her mind next. "I know we're all glad that Judy and Danny got married. But I have been struggling with this aching doubt about how long it will last."

"Really?" her mother said in dismay. "Why is that?"

"Oh, I don't know." Marge wondered if she should have even started this conversation. "I was just thinking about that story I told you before about what happened with Danny and that scuzzy girl at the bar. Leopards don't usually change their spots. And Danny doesn't really have the best of track records. He doesn't have the best reputation either."

Carla stopped wiping the table to look Marge gently in the eyes. "Thank God that He gives us extra chances to make changes for the better. I've been praying over this whole situation, and I really believe that Danny wants to make good with Judy. He agreed to marry her in the church with an alcohol-free wedding party. Those are some pretty significant changes. I also think that his eyes must have been opened up about the blessings of having a baby. And I think he really wants to see his son grow up."

"Oh, I guess I was just being cynical," Marge said as she thoughtfully went back to work. "Do you think that the fact that his father died while heading to the hospital to see the baby meant something to Danny? Or maybe it somehow opened his eyes?"

"Hm-mh," her mother considered. "I never really thought about that. But there might be something to that."

Marge continued, "A few months ago, Danny was at our insurance office putting in a claim for some damage on his bike, and I took the opportunity to tell him how happy I was to not be working in the bar anymore, and how I thought drinking messed up Dad and made life so difficult for us at home."

They glanced at each other and Marge continued. "Sorry, Mom. I wasn't trying to make you feel bad. But anyway, I also mentioned that I thought his father had a problem with drinking. Then I even suggested to Danny that maybe he should to look at his own drinking as well."

Carla smiled with pride at Marge. "I'm very pleased and proud of you for talking to Danny that way. Who knows? Maybe you contributed somehow to his coming to his senses. Maybe even that's why he agreed to the alcohol-free wedding. As I said before, God gives us lots of chances to do better."

They both kept quietly working for a few minutes while Marge contemplated how to approach her mother about moving back home. It seemed like a good idea because if she moved back in with her mother, neither of them would have to live alone. And it would also save them both money. It would take some swallowing of pride because Marge felt sort of bad about the way she treated her mother when she moved out.

"Mom, I have to admit that I've learned a few things in the past year or so."

Carla could see that something big was about to be disclosed, and she wanted to be as encouraging as possible. "Like what, honey?"

"Well, like what a great mom you've been. And how much I regret getting so angry with you and moving out the way I did. I'm really sorry I was such a stupid, mean kid."

"Really? Well, Marge, it seems like you've done a lot of growing this past year. And don't worry. It's okay. I forgive you. I know I wasn't always perfect either."

"You know what, Mom? I wanted to tell you something else. It doesn't make sense for me to be paying rent when I could be living at home with you and helping you out with the upkeep. Plus, it would be saving us both money."

Carla and Bill both gave each other a startled look. Then they both walked toward Marge. Marge knew they had something serious to say to her, and she had an idea what it might be. But she wasn't completely sure it was something she wanted to hear.

Bill put his arm around Carla's shoulder as he said, "I know you wanted to wait, Carla, but I think now is a good time to tell her."

Carla put down what was in her hands and put her arm around Bill's waist. "Marge, Bill and I have been talking about this for a few months now. We were thinking about announcing it today, but then we decided to wait. But I guess at this point, I have no choice but to tell you that we've decided to get married."

Marge was rather stunned. She knew they were seeing each other and had an idea it might be coming, but she wasn't completely prepared for this. She fumbled for words. Then, after a couple of seconds, she returned to her senses. "Well, congratulations to both of you."

"Marge," Carla paused and then went on, "you can still move back home."

Marge was puzzled, "With you and Bill?"

"Well, actually, I was thinking about selling the house, and I haven't really run this idea past Bill yet. But either I could keep it, and you could live next door to us. Or, maybe if Bill didn't mind, you could move into Bill's house with us."

"You mean you're moving into Bill's house?"

"Yes, I'm moving into Bill's house."

Carla could see the confusion she created.

"Bill's house is probably the better choice of the two since it is a little bigger and in better condition."

Bill spoke up. "Carla, honey, let's not make life complicated. Marge, it doesn't make sense to have two houses when we can all comfortably live in just one. I know you weren't too fond of me before because I started seeing your mother very shortly after your father died, and I think you thought it was a little too soon. Isn't that right?"

Marge's eyes opened wide with embarrassment.

He continued on, "Well, I understand how you felt, but the truth is that I've always admired your mother for what a wonderful woman she was. She is not only a beautiful lady, but she is a wonderful person."

Marge looked down, still embarrassed. "You're right. My mother is a great person."

Bill walked over closer to where Marge was working and stood next to her until she looked up at him. "It's okay, Marge. I really do understand how you felt, and maybe even feel now. I hope you don't mind having me for a stepfather." He paused and then continued. "In the meantime, my two sons are both married and moved out on their own. So there's plenty of room in the house, and I think your mother and I would be very happy to have you living with us. Does that sound acceptable to you, Marge?"

Carla smiled with pleasure at Bill. Bill lovingly smiled back at her.

Marge swallowed with shame. "Bill, I really thought you were just *making moves* on my mother. I didn't know you thought so highly of her and would eventually marry her. I feel kind of bad that you know I thought so badly of you."

Bill reassured her, "It's okay, Marge. I understand. It's not easy for a kid when her father dies and some guy pursues her mother shortly after." Then he asked her again, "Would you like to live with your mother and me? We would both be very glad to have you living with us."

"Since you put it that way," Marge's face was blushing a little, "Yes, I would."

Carla took Bill's hand and looked into his face with a smile, "With God, all things work toward the good."

Bill smiled back at her, "For those who love Him."

"Oh, wow! Are you two quoting Scripture verses to each other?" Marge laughingly complained.

They obviously were. So, all three of them broke out in laughter.

"Is that why you two hit it off so well together?" Marge remarked, "You're both Bible-quoting Holy Rollers!"

Bill cocked his head to the side with a quizzical look on his face and asked her, "Bible-quoting Holy Roller? Oh my! Well, is that really so bad?"

Marge thoughtfully surrendered. "No. Actually, I think it's good!" she said as she smiled peacefully. After all the years of resisting, she finally accepted that her mother's approach to life was good all along. It was obvious that for Marge a healing had taken place. She realized that all along it was not her mother or Bill that needed to be forgiven. It was her that needed to be forgiven. "I didn't realize how much I didn't understand," she confessed. "But, I do now. I'm so glad you both forgive me, and I'm just amazed and so happy at how things have worked out for all of us. Life is really going to be good now—for everyone."

CHAPTER 23

A Better Life

The weekend after Judy and Danny returned from the shore, life and possessions got moved all around, and life seemed topsy-turvy. Judy and Kevin were moving out of the cottage and into the Schisler residence, while Marge was preparing for the move into the Bach residence. Her mother and Bill were planning to get married in only a couple of months, so it wouldn't be long before Marge and her mother would be moving too. In the meantime, Marge decided to get rid of some things and start boxing up a few other things to go into Bill's basement.

On Friday nights, the bank was open until late. So the Friday after Judy and Kevin were done moving, Danny and Judy were finally able to find time to go to the bank together to close his old accounts and open new accounts jointly in both of their names. The bank was quite a few blocks away, but it was a warm beautiful night, and they decided to walk. They bundled little Kevin into his baby carriage, gathered all their papers, and headed for the bank.

When they got to the bank, they saw a desk in a back room with a sign on the door saying *Clifton Lang Fuller IV, President*. A man was sitting behind the desk with two other men sitting outside the door waiting for an appointment with him. Danny and Judy just decided to sit down and wait.

Judy remembered that Cindy Boyer worked at this bank. She also remembered how humiliated Cindy made her feel that day in the drugstore. *I hope she gets to see me now*, she thought to herself. *I'll be sure to flash my engagement ring in front of her.*

A woman's voice came up behind her and Danny, and asked, "Hello. Can I help you? Mr. Fuller is going to be busy for a while."

"Yes. Thanks." Danny stood up. "We just got married, and we want to change our accounts to joint accounts."

The lady was Mrs. Moody, Mr. Fuller's secretary. Judy remembered when Mrs. Moody was a teller, and her mother would take her to the bank with her to do bank transactions. She would set Judy up on the ledge so Judy could see everything that was going on. Then she would chit-chat with Mrs. Moody if there wasn't a line behind her.

Mrs. Moody looked at their marriage license and birth certificates and exclaimed, "Judy Brennan. Well, I'll be! Are you Carla's little girl?" Mrs. Moody asked.

"I sure am," Judy laughingly replied.

"My goodness, it's been so long since I've seen you. Why, you were just a little girl when I saw you last."

"Can you imagine that?" Judy giggled. "And now I'm grown up with my own baby, and I'm married. I guess I should formally introduce you to my husband, Danny, and our baby, Kevin."

"Pleased to meet you." Dan introduced himself, "Dan Schisler."

"So good to meet you, Dan." Then she turned to Judy, "Can I hold the baby?"

After some small talk about how everyone was doing, they sat down to complete all the paperwork for the new accounts. When they finished with all their business, they chatted some more.

Judy was burning with curiosity. "Do you still have a girl working in the drive-up named Cindy Boyer?"

"Is she your friend?" Mrs. Moody asked with a concerned look on her face.

"Well, not really." Judy looked puzzled. "But I do know her, and I was just wondering how she was doing."

"Oh! I thought you must have heard."

"Heard what?" Judy was now even more puzzled.

Mrs. Moody realized it would be awkward if she didn't continue with the news. "Listen, since I know you, I'm going to tell you. But you're not to tell a soul that I told you this, okay?"

Judy knew something juicy was about to be disclosed. "Okay, I promise. We won't tell a soul. Right, Danny?"

Danny just smirked with interest.

"We had to let her go a while ago."

"Oh really!" Judy seemed surprised.

"Yes, she was caught taking money from her cash drawer."

"Wow! That's unbelievable. What a shame to lose her job like that," Judy tried to sound sincere as she thought to herself, *How do you like that? After she bragged so much that day at the pharmacy and had the nerve to put me down like she did.*

On their way home, Judy pondered how good her life was now. Especially after all those months of wishing she could just die or go back and do things all over differently. It all worked out good after all. She had her home with Danny, whom she loved so much, and they had their adorable little baby, Kevin. She was just amazed at how much her life had turned around. *There's hope for everyone*, she thought.

When they stopped at the corner waiting for the red light to change, they heard Freddie Dietz's voice hollering down the block at them. "Hey, you two! Wait up! I'll walk with you." He ran halfway down the block until he caught up to them. "How ya doing, old man?" He pat Danny on the back, and they shook hands. Then he pecked Judy a kiss on the cheek. "How ya doing, sweetheart?"

Their conversation was cheerful and light as they continued on their way. They shared their amazement over the events that had taken place in the past year. Then Fred said to Dan, "You know what? They are really missing you down at Custer's."

Danny flicked his cigarette butt out into the street as he blew out its last puff of smoke. "Remember that toast you gave at the wedding, Fred?"

"Yeah," Fred replied.

"Well, you were right. You did lose a pool partner because I won't be going to the bar anymore." Then Dan smiled down at little Kevin in the baby carriage. "Fred, you're still my best friend but no more visits to Custer's. We have decided we're rising above what we grew up with. We mean nothing against our parents. They did the best they could with what they had, and I'm sure you know I loved my dad. But we just want something better for our family." Then he looked at Judy, and they both smiled lovingly at each other.